Praise for Ben Vendetta

"A blast from the post-punk past that brings back mid-eighties Britain in one wired, synaptic rush, a coming-of-age story that is as poignant, political, hormonal and hilarious as the sounds it celebrates."

—Cathi Unsworth, author of *Weirdo*, *Bad Penny Blues*, *The Singer*

"It's an addictive read, an affirmative and faithful story of sex, drugs and rock & roll. Where an equivalent novel such as Nick Hornby's *High Fidelity* becomes evermore unrealistic to get to its happy ending, *Wivenhoe Park* retains a believable optimism through sheer faith in rock & roll.

—Paul Rayson, *Muso's Guide*

"I enjoyed *Wivenhoe Park* thoroughly. Ben Vendetta captures the youth feel and mood of those times quite vividly."

—Sam Knee, author of *A Scene In Between*

"This is classic coming of age stuff. Drew makes friends, hangs out with bands, dates inappropriate girls, takes drugs and whole lot more. But what makes *Wivenhoe Park* such a joy is that Ben writes in a very engaging way ... If you ever enjoyed *High Fidelity*, went to a British university in the mid-'80s or are counting the days until Cherry Red reissues the legendary C86 compilation, you'll love this."

—*PopJunkie*

"Vendetta brings back an '80s era when a stunning, now-legendary post-punk/indie rock scene was blazing in Britain, yet this time, unlike with punk rock, a smaller slice of Americans followed its brilliance. He slyly evokes this in a coming-of-college-age story of throwing off the influence (and snares) of normal Middle American life by instead immersing himself into the thick of the NME/Melody Maker/Sounds-fed maelstrom in England itself."

—Jack Rabid, *The Big Takeover*

"If John Hughes were still alive… well… he'd never touch this story. It's too full of the sort of gritty realism that never made it into his well-scrubbed coming-of-age stories."

—Robert Cherry (former Editor-in-Chief, *Alternative Press*)

"For those of us who came of age in the '80s and didn't give a hoot about bands like Foreigner or Poison but instead wanted REAL music then *Wivenhoe Park* will be a real page turner that's hard to put down. It certainly was for me."

—Tim Hinely, *Dagger*

"*Wivenhoe Park* wrenched me back to a mid-'80s Britain where punk was dead and alternative/goth ruled. If birds, booze and Bunnymen are your thing, as they are mine, then dust off your Sisters of Mercy LPs, squeeze into your *Meat Is Murder* T-shirt and enjoy the ride."

—Dave Hawes (Catherine Wheel)

"Ben Vendetta takes you back to a simpler time when culture and relationships were complicated but fun, and when music really mattered to your life. This dive into historical fiction is like a post-punk version of *High Fidelity*, with a bit more grit, sass, and reality. It's a great read.

—Tony Schinella (Award-winning journalist, broadcaster; musician)

"*Wivenhoe Park* brings you back to that rollercoaster ride of your early 20s. Every great new discovery — music, friends, food, drinking, the opposite sex — is like a match to dynamite. Every disappointment is the end of the world. With each experience, Drew grows just a little bit. In the end, he's figured out who he is, what he can give to the world, and what it takes to be a great partner and friend."

—Michelle Briand, WXRV (The River)

Heartworm

Heartworm

Ben Vendetta

COOPERATIVE TRADE

an imprint of Cooperative Press

Heartworm

ISBN 13: 978-1-937513-72-6

First edition published by Cooperative Trade, a division of Cooperative Press

www.cooperativepress.com

Text © 2015, Ben Vendetta

Cover art © 2015, Arabella Proffer

If you have questions or comments about this book, or need information about licensing, custom editions, special sales, or academic/corporate purchases, please contact Cooperative Press: info@cooperativepress.com or 13000 Athens Ave C288, Lakewood, OH 44107 USA

Twinkle

I'm on holiday in London, nursing a Scotch at the all night bar in the Columbia Hotel. The establishment is usually a hedonistic hotspot for touring bands and groupies, but tonight the room is empty, the atmosphere dead. And it's far too bright, like a casino, not a good place to lose oneself in thought and drink. Several inebriated Geordies standing to my right claim to have been on the piss for the better part of a day. Hard men with grizzled faces and indistinguishable accents, uniformly dressed in black and white striped Newcastle United jerseys. They leave me alone when it becomes clear that I don't give a fuck about the English Premier League. I eye up a group of photogenic Japanese mods, politely seated at a corner table, cameras on the ready, no doubt desperate for a chance meeting with Liam Gallagher or Damon Albarn. One of the girls has impossibly perfect pink hair and beautiful silky smooth skin. I contemplate approaching her, reminded of an old Deep Purple song. I wonder if my fantasy girl is from Tokyo and, better yet, if she'd be good to me.

I feel a tap on my shoulder and turn my head.

"Is that you, Drew?" he asks.

He's about my height. A good-looking man with neatly cropped blonde hair, expensively dressed in a black cashmere V-neck jumper and designer jeans. He's with a bleached blonde, whose sexy body is squeezed into a tight red T-shirt that says *Enjoy Cocaine* in the same cursive font as the iconic Coca-Cola logo. Her black skirt barely covers her ass and I don't know how she can walk in such high heels.

"Yeah, I'm Drew," I say, struggling to put a name to the face.

"It's Dave, mate."

"Jesus," I say, now remembering.

"How long has it been?" he asks.

"Nearly ten years."

Dave was from Manchester. A cool cat with a pompadour and sideburns that put Morrissey to shame. We were close friends when we were students at the University of Essex, until he slept with Julie, the girl I was with before Claire and I got together. Ancient history.

"This is Rachel," he says, pointing to the young tart. "Rachel Blitz."

I do a double take. The blonde is the publicist responsible for breaking a number of trendy British groups. Chances are you own a record or two touched by the hand of Blitz.

"Nice to meet you, Drew," she says. "Are you in a band?"

People often assume I'm a musician because my hair is long and I'm smack addict thin.

"Drew's a journo," says Dave. "Hot Press and Spin. He even got a piece published in Melody Maker when he was still at university. Talented bastard. He's about the only Yank who gets what's going on over here."

I'm shocked that Dave has kept tabs on me, that he's followed my career. Rachel goes into full publicist mode when she learns I'm a writer.

"Have you listened to Concealer?" she asks. "I just started working with them. They're like a cross between the Jam and Blur."

She reaches into her purse and hands me a CD. The cover shot features four young lads drinking tea at an authentic roadside café. They look sharp in their skinny Merc suits, smug grins on their faces.

"They're playing tomorrow at Camden Centre with the Bluetones," she says. "It's going to be mental. There's an after party at Blow Up, too. You must come. I'll put you on the guest list."

"Sure," I say.

"So what's your connection?" I ask Dave.

"I'm Concealer's manager. First saw them about a year ago. Felt like I was McGee discovering Oasis."

Dave goes on to tell me that he worked in banking for five years after leaving university. Then he inherited a fortune when his grandfather died, so he moved to London and invested money in real estate, buying up cheap properties in areas about to become gentrified.

"Fix 'em up and sell 'em for a massive profit," he says. "I was making enough that I didn't have to work anymore, so I started going to gigs again. You know, like we used to at Essex. I have a few acts on my roster now."

"Like who?" I ask.

"I'm working with a group out of Manchester called Northern Uproar. They're just kids, but they're fucking brilliant. They've signed to Heavenly Records. James Dean

Bradfield from Manic Street Preachers is producing their album."

Dave asks what I'm drinking and I say any Scotch will do. He orders something top shelf for both of us. He and Rachel start namedropping. First, they talk about what a sound lad Bradfield is—I can't help but wonder how many of the Manics Rachel has slept with—and then Dave tells me how he's become mates with Noel Gallagher.

"Liam can be a bit of a cunt," says Dave, "but Noel's a proper geezer." He downs his Scotch and slams it on the bar.

"You're a proper geezer, too, Drew," he says. "It's nice to know we're both working in music after all these years. I remember we used to talk about things like that." The Scotch is making him emotional. He even wipes back a tear.

"This is so sweet," says Rachel, clasping her hands. "I love happy reunions."

We move to a table and Rachel orders another round. Dave asks about Claire. I tell him that she left me four months ago, just before summer fell, running off to Glastonbury with her lover, a hippie sculptor named Sean.

"Poor boy," says Rachel.

"I'll live."

She edges closer to me, like a vulture circling a carcass. I know she doesn't give a fuck about my welfare, but I don't care. She's paying for the drinks.

"Dave and I will take care of you," she says. "How long are you in London?"

"Just a few more days. Then it's back to Dublin."

We have another round.

"I still feel shitty about how you and I fell out at university," says Dave.

"Me, too," I say. "Pretty dumb in retrospect. Whatever happened to Julie, anyway?"

"You don't know?"

"I guess not."

"She stayed on at Essex for another year to get a master's degree and ended up meeting some Yank. They got married. I don't know where she's living now."

I don't pursue it. I'm more preoccupied with the present. Rachel's stroking my thigh. I return the favor. Her skin is soft. Sensing what's going on, Dave says he should get home before his wife kills him. We say our goodbyes and Rachel and I go to my room, which, based on the fading floral wallpaper and puke green carpet, was last decorated in the mid-seventies. She excuses herself to the bathroom and returns a few minutes later in nothing but heels and thong panties, striking a seductive pose, hands crisscrossing her breasts like a Russ Meyer super vixen.

The sex is fast and dirty, but somehow mechanical, like she's doing her make up. Rachel has a gutter mouth. I can barely keep up.

"That was hot," she says when we're through. "It's like we have some kind of animal magnetism."

"Animal nitrate," I say.

We soon fall asleep. A few hours later the Boo Radleys wake me up, telling me it's a beautiful morning. I groan. I hate this song. I used to like them but these days Martin

Carr is writing hits for housewives. I feel like Bill Murray in *Groundhog Day*, tortured daily by Sonny and Cher. Rachel, on the other hand, is full of energy, wired up like she's done a line of coke. Maybe she has? She hands me a cup of tea.

"I need to get going soon, love," she says. "Lots to do before the concert."

The new Blur single "Country House" comes on next. I feel like throwing the radio through the window, but turn down the volume instead. I follow Rachel into the shower and we have a quick fuck before she leaves.

That evening I meet Dave, Rachel, and the Concealer lads for dinner and drinks at a Pizza Hut of all places. For some bizarre reason the second-tier American chain is considered upscale in England, down to its proper service and quality wine list. They're all pissed when I arrive, and I can see white stuff on the singer Ace's nose—yes, he's called Ace. I spot two pies with uniquely British toppings on the table; one has chicken and mushrooms, the other an odd combination of veggies, including sweet corn. I grab a slice of the former as Rachel tells the band that I write for Spin.

"Whatcha think of the single then, mate?" asks Ace.

"I really like it," I say, not wanting to tell him that it sounds like a bad Blur song, exaggerated Mockney vocals and all. I could barely get through it when I gave it a spin earlier in the day.

"I like the B-Side, too," I go on. "Shows a more sensitive side like the Small Faces 'Afterglow' or something."

Lying to bands and publicists has become second nature to me. Rock 'n' roll used to feel pure, but being in the industry for so long has soured me on it. The best song I've heard all year is "I Hate Rock 'n' Roll" by the Jesus and Mary Chain. It's a vengeful attack on the music business. Near the end, the singer Jim Reid spits out in disgust: "I hate rock 'n' roll. I hate it cause its fucks with my soul." Lethal stuff. These new pretenders like Oasis, Blur, and Concealer aren't coming from dark places like that. Punk was supposed to have buried the coke and limo lifestyles of the seventies, but now it's returned full circle.

Ace is thrilled by my critique. "I fookin' love the Faces," he says. "This bloke gets it, Rachel. He knows what we're on about." He's happy as a chimp.

The Concealer gig is fun. Dave and I watch from the bar, supping our pints while the kids dance up a storm. The mod revival is back. I've never seen so much Fred Perry and Ben Sherman gear in one place; a few lads are even wearing suits. So many cute girls, too. I wonder if I'll get off with Rachel again. Tonight she's wearing a tight black and silver Pulp T-shirt, another micro-mini skirt. I'm getting aroused watching her bounce up and down on the dance floor.

After the gig Dave takes me to the Good Mixer, an Irish dive bar that's become a haven for bands and scenesters. Within minutes I've spotted members of Blur, Elastica, Pulp, and Suede holding court. I feel out of place, like I've crashed a country club shindig or perhaps, in this case, barged in on an English schoolboy circle jerk. Suede singer Brett Anderson is channeling his inner Bowie, sucking on a cigarette like a glamorous drag queen. Every few seconds he flicks back his hair. He looks even thinner in real life than on television or on the multiple magazine covers he graces—almost anorexic. Dave introduces me to Alex James from Blur, who seems likeable enough until Dave tries to curry favor. Alex not quite sincerely promises to put in a good word for Concealer then makes a quick escape. Dave continues his meet-and-greet escapades with other members of the Britpop contingent while I slink off to have a pint at the bar. I enjoy a moment of solitude until a suddenly energized Dave—I wonder if he's done a line—tracks me down, saying it's time for Blow Up. As I follow him out the door, I hear someone heckle Pulp's singer, Jarvis Cocker, telling him his band are shit. Part of me wants to stay, intrigued by the first sign of discord I've seen, but Dave is already a few strides ahead of me, motoring along like a race walker.

Blow Up is at a multiple level venue called The Laurel Tree. The atmosphere downstairs is mellow with old soul on the decks, but the upstairs room swings like a dinosaur's dick. The DJ is mixing in punk classics with all the new hits, including a track from the forthcoming Oasis album. It sounds monstrous. Liam snarls like Johnny Rotten, only he isn't spitting vitriol at the Queen—he's celebrating his new found wealth. "All your dreams are made when you're chained to your mirror with your razor blade." It's the sonic equivalent of *Scarface*, the guitars roaring like helicopters in *Apocalypse Now*. Right there and then I have an epiphany that Oasis might become the biggest band on the planet, and it bothers me. Dave pumps his fist in the air, shouting something in my ear about youth culture finally winning. I wish I could agree with him—maybe even do a celebratory line to seal the deal—but my more sensible side just wants to throw up.

It's déjà vu. In the early eighties my friends and I were teased (a few even beaten up) by conservative Reagan youth for our haircuts and "strange" clothes, constantly peppered with derogatory insults like "art fag." A half decade later those same jocks were rocking out to R.E.M., U2, and the Cure, who had all become mainstream in

America. Something similar happened in England. A few years ago, bands like Suede, the Auteurs, and Denim were sporting thrift shop clothes and tackling social class structure in their songs. Hell, Suede even wanted to chase the dragon. Now it's morphed into Britpop. Cool Britannia. Lads' music. Tonight feels like a Loaded magazine bash; football hooligans turned rockers in designer clobber crashing the art school party. I walk to the bar and notice Rachel in the corner with Ace. I don't care enough to confront her. I say goodbye to Dave, who tries to cheer me up by referring to Rachel as a dirty slag. As I descend the stairs I bump into Johnny and Chris from Menswear. They're fixing their hair and adjusting their suit lapels, readying themselves for a grand entrance. Their hit single "Daydreamer" is now playing and I can't help but wonder if this is some perfectly choreographed stunt arranged by their record label.

The next day, hung over as fuck, I decide to do some record shopping. I take the tube to Oxford Circus Station and make my way to Berwick Street in Soho. It's one of my favorite spots in London, an eclectic mix of trendy boutiques, market stalls, record shops, and a bit further down the road, advertising firms and sex shops. It's probably no coincidence that the latter two are located in such close proximity. In a few weeks, the neighborhood will become forever immortalized on the front cover of the new Oasis album *(What's The Story) Morning Glory?*

As I'm poking aimlessly through stacks of CDs and vinyl at my favorite haunt, Sister Ray Records, mournful cello music slowly rises from the speakers. A stunning melody and Joy Division-like bass line follows suit. The singer's words are pure Bukowski, something about a girl turning tricks just like her mother. "She's the air I breathe, not too pure for me," the voice says. "She's the air I breathe, not too cheap for me." It all kicks in on the chorus; a tsunami of crushing guitars and a line repeated ad nauseam: "She's the only one for me now and always." This group, whoever they are, sound like an impossibly glorious mish mash of Velvet Underground, My Bloody Valentine, and Echo and the Bunnymen.

I rush to the counter, startling the clerk, who's lost in a magazine. He's wearing a faded Spacemen 3 T-shirt, a fellow traveler. Surely, he understands. I ask who's responsible for the glorious racket.

"Whipping Boy," he says, looking up from the article he's reading. Something about the forthcoming Blur and Oasis albums. Blur versus Oasis. The new Battle of Britain.

"You mean the band from Dublin?" I say, not quite sure I heard him right. It can't be.

"That's the one, mate. It's their new single 'Twinkle,'" he says, handing me the jewel case. "The album is brilliant. A mate of mine at the NME has an advance. It will be out at the end of October."

I'm speechless. I know these guys. I feel proud. I interviewed Whipping Boy for Hot Press when their debut Submarine was released in '92. Unlike most Dublin bands of the time, they weren't enamored with U2 or R.E.M., preferring the noisy sounds of Big Black, Jesus and Mary Chain, My Bloody Valentine, and Sonic Youth. Some people slated them for sounding too much like the latter.

Their live performances were legendary. People would tell me stories of how the singer Fearghal McKee would strip naked on stage and cut himself with broken bottles. Iggy Pop kind of stuff. I never saw him get that out of control, but as a Michigan boy, who grew up idolizing the Stooges, I was impressed by his conviction. The last time I saw them they were on fire, as breathtaking as the Mary Chain or My Bloody Valentine. Fearghal appeared to be in a trance, gazing straight into the crowd with the intensity of a boxer staring down his opponent. Whippet-thin guitarist Paul Page was lost in a world of his own, conjuring up mighty effects and chords that were part Thurston Moore and part Kevin Shields. The bass player Myles McDonnell, with his handsome Jared Leto looks, was channeling his inner Peter Hook, playing with even more swagger than usual, while the drummer Colm Hassett coolly kept beat. Near the end of the set Fearghal charged into the crowd, driving his head into an unfortunate punter's gut.

"Twinkle" is the best single I've heard in years. I don't think I've been so floored by a band since first hearing the Mary Chain. I listen to the song at least a half dozen times that afternoon on my Discman, obsessing over Fearghal's words. "Waiting to be bled, turning tricks just like your mother. Left my dreams for dead, making out with every other." I wonder if he crossed paths with a girl like Rachel Blitz, or, for that matter, Claire.

The Ryanair flight to Dublin is rocky. There's lots of turbulence and the plane keeps screeching. I'm convinced it will blow up mid-air. I regret not spending the extra cash on British Air or Aer Lingus as I try to hold in the Big Mac I scarfed down at Heathrow. We land hard on the tarmac and the little girl across the aisle throws up on her father's lap. I turn away before I do the same. Welcome to Dublin.

Favourite Sister

As much as I love the adrenaline rush of London, I'm glad to be back in Dublin. The city resonates with me: the sea, the greenery, the Wicklow Mountains to the south, and the people. I thought Claire and I would remain here forever, but now that she's gone I can barely pay the rent. My older brother Paul has been pleading with me to come back to America. He's a professor at Harvard and will begin a sabbatical at Stanford in January. He asked if I might want to housesit his condo. Like everyone else I know, Paul has given up on the idea that Claire is coming back. The day after I return from London I phone him and take him up on his offer. I feel sad and a little sick, but I'm tired of waiting for miracles.

In addition to writing, which provides a rather paltry income, I've been working at a non-profit organization called Cooperation North. We organize workshops that bring together Catholic and Protestant children in Northern Ireland. As an editor, I don't attend these events, but interview the facilitators who do, writing reports for newsletters, magazines, and grant proposals. Northern Ireland is so segregated that it's not unusual for kids growing up there to have never met someone from another faith. It's also extremely dangerous, even with the current Irish Republican Army ceasefire. The levels of violence have gone down considerably in comparison to the peak years of the Troubles, but the threat of future escalation is always present. Belfast, in particular, is a scary place. British troops and tanks line the streets and, even, department stores, like Marks & Spencer, are guarded by soldiers in full riot gear.

Claire grew up in an integrated neighborhood near Queen's University, where her father teaches. She's a Protestant but not a unionist. The unionists want Northern Ireland to remain part of Great Britain. The nationalists, who are Catholic and whose violent wing is represented by the IRA, want the six counties of Ulster to integrate with the Republic of Ireland. I find the Catholics in Dublin to be relatively indifferent to the mess up north, paying only lip service to the cause.

My colleague Siobhan is a nationalist. She doesn't support the armed struggle, but she sympathizes with it. She's young, blonde, and beautiful; three years out of University College, Dublin. She's also mad about American music, especially Dinosaur, Jr., the Pixies, and Pavement. We became instant friends. It was during her first week at Co-operation North. She was in the break room, reading Hot Press, the issue with my Whipping Boy feature.

"I write for Hot Press," I boasted as I walked by. Don't judge, we've all been there.

She looked up and smiled. "Are you in this issue?" she asked.

I stood behind her and slowly turned the pages for her until I located the piece.

"I like Whipping Boy," she said. "They remind me of Sonic Youth. I have one of their EPs. I just heard 'Favourite Sister' on the Dave Fanning Show. It's brilliant."

We ended up talking for the rest of the lunch break. I felt guilty that I was flirting so heavily, but it was a rush to talk to someone who was so passionate about music. Claire used to be that way, but once she started pursuing a Ph.D.

at Trinity she lost interest. She thought it was silly that I still wanted to see bands, let alone write about them. Claire stopped going to concerts with me, so I started to hang out with Siobhan. I felt sleazy, like I was having an affair. I'd tell Claire I was going out alone, even though I planned to meet Siobhan at some pub or club. I didn't disclose this friendship to Claire because she would have flipped out, even though it was completely platonic. Siobhan was a popular girl on the local scene, always dating musicians in up and coming bands. These relationships never seemed to work out and I became a shoulder to cry on. Eventually, I opened up to her and told her about my troubles with Claire. She was the first person I told when Claire left me.

Siobhan took me out for dinner and drinks that evening and the two of us got sloshed. She was upset with her latest flame, an impossibly handsome bleached blonde gunslinger named Pat, who played guitar in a band called Flash. Pat is a wanker—a lot of the guys on the scene call him Pat the Almighty behind his back—but the girls all seem to love him. Siobhan told me that she and Pat slept together a few times before he stopped returning calls. A girlfriend saw him out with another woman.

"I really pick the winners, don't I?"

"You'll find someone right for you," I said. "You're a beautiful girl."

"Do you mean that?"

"Of course."

We were standing on the platform at Tara Street Station, waiting for our train. My flat is in Ballsbridge and Siobhan lives with her mother in Blackrock, a few stops further down the line. I was loaded and lonely.

"You're a good man for saying that, Drew," she said. "Claire's a fool to have left you."

"I guess I wasn't good enough for her."

"Don't be so sad, Drew."

She kissed me softly and I returned the favor. We made out for about a minute, until she pulled away abruptly.

"I'm sorry, Drew. That's the last thing we need right now. You're vulnerable and I'm sad. Let's not spoil our friendship."

A few days later she got back together with Pat the Almighty.

Siobhan's at the office when I come back from London. She's wearing an unbuttoned flannel over a black tank top, jeans, and Doc Martens boots.

"How was your trip?" she asks.

I give her the rundown, including my encounter with Rachel Blitz. The two of us share everything—I know far too much about Siobhan's dalliances with assorted young (and not so young) Dublin musicians.

"Yuck," she says, in reference to Rachel.

"I know, but I did use a condom."

She laughs. "So was that your first time… you know after Claire?"

"Yeah."

"I'll buy you a pint at lunch to celebrate."

I smile. "I can drink to that."

"Seriously though you look good. You were so miserable this summer, Drew."

"I know, and now I'm sad for a different reason. I'm leaving."

"Leaving this job?"

"Leaving Dublin." I tell Siobhan about my brother's offer.

"That's so sad," she says. "I'm heartbroken. I'm going to miss you so much."

At lunchtime we go to a pub near St. Stephen's Green. She buys me a Guinness. She's drinking orange juice.

"Rough night?" I ask.

"No," she whispers, pointing to her stomach. "I just found out last week. It's only been fifteen weeks, so please don't tell anyone."

"Congratulations. Is Pat the father?" I feel hesitant to ask, knowing her history, but I can't remember her mentioning anyone else.

"Yes," she says.

"How did he take it?"

"Not too well at first. He wanted me to take care of it. You know, go to England and get an abortion, but now he's resigned to do his best. He called yesterday and said he wants to be a good father. We're not getting married or anything. I don't even want to live with him. I have my doubts that he'll even stay involved, but I want to have the child. It feels right."

An old Byrds song comes on, "Turn! Turn! Turn!" She

sings along. "California Dreaming" is next. "I love those sixties songs," she says. "They make me happy. My mum has a lot of old records. She told me my father was a music fan, but I never knew him. He left when I was a toddler."

"So you've never talked to him?"

"No," she says. "I don't know him at all, but I suppose he'll be forever tied to my mum. It's the curse of Ireland. No divorce, no rights for women. We're controlled by angry old men and bumpkin religion."

I phone Claire, telling her about my plans, begging her to reconsider. Come to America, I say, it will be a fresh start for both of us. She tells me she's happy, that this is the life she wants. I'm not sure I believe her. Maybe I just don't want to, but she sounds cold and distant, as if she's reading from a script. She's definitely fallen for Sean's new age babble.

"We're not on the same plane anymore," she says. "You're too attached to the material world. I need to be with someone who embraces his spiritual side."

Siobhan invites me to a New Year's party at Pat's flat. She tells me that Pat is going to move to Blackrock to live with her and her mother and help raise the child. He's up to his old tricks when I get there though, banging out ballads on an acoustic to a small audience of fawning females. During a particularly cringeworthy rendition of U2's "One," Siobhan leaves the room in a huff. I follow her outside and ask if she's okay. She seems flustered.

"I don't know why I get so mad at these things," she says. "It's just that everyone I fall for ends up leaving me. I don't trust Pat. I want to be someone's only one. Is that too much to hope for?"

"No, it's not," I say. I feel rotten. She's twenty-four, pregnant, and forever tied to a wanker musician. Part of me wants to rescue her, save her, but then it dawns on me that maybe I'm not much better than Pat. What the fuck have I done with my life?

"I wish you didn't have to go, Drew."

"I wish I didn't either, but I need to leave Dublin. I have too many bad memories here. I need a fresh start."

"I understand. I wish I could go with you. Doesn't J. Mascis from Dinosaur, Jr. live in Massachusetts?"

We both laugh and the mood lightens. It's almost midnight. When the clock strikes twelve, Siobhan and I kiss. We don't let it linger like we did during our drunken session on the train platform. It's just a quick peck, but it feels real and I feel sad for what could have been.

"I'm going to miss you Siobhan," I say. "Will you be okay?"

She smiles. "Yes. You know me, Drew. I'm a survivor. True Irish blue."

Switchblade Smile

It's January and I'm celebrating my thirty-first birthday alone at my brother's condo in Cambridge, suffering from severe cabin fever. The last person I spoke to since landing at Logan Airport three days ago was the door guy at my new building who handed over the keys with a scowl. I crack open a bottle of wine and skim through the Boston Phoenix, the local alternative weekly. The new Whipping Boy album is playing on the stereo. Appropriately titled *Heartworm*, the record is an achingly honest portrayal of life, love, and loss. I've never heard anything so heartrending. The wine's kicking in and I feel content to stay indoors, soak in the sounds, and take in my new surroundings.

Paul's condo is exactly what you'd expect from a recently divorced, upwardly mobile guy in his mid-thirties. The living room is decorated with leather furniture, a glass coffee table, and far too much chrome. Framed French film posters adorn the walls in place of the original art that his ex, Caroline, liberated. There's a huge television with a built-in VCR player, a high-end Bose stereo with surround sound, and a vast collection of classical CDs, fastidiously arranged on a custom-built shelf. His bookshelf is even more impressive, an extensive library containing political science and history books relevant to his research and a surprising amount of fiction. I never knew that he read for fun.

Paul said that I could use his bedroom, which has a sliding door that leads to a balcony with an impressive Boston skyline view, but I've camped out in the sparse guest room instead. There's barely enough space for a futon and a dresser, but I feel more at home in tight quarters. I didn't take much with me when I left Ireland, having sold all of the furniture from the Ballsbridge flat, plus most of my books and music. The only possessions I own at the moment are a suitcase full of clothes and a selection of CDs I couldn't part with.

I take a sip of wine and lose myself in melancholy. It's funny how a man's relationship with alcohol and drugs changes over the years. When we're young it's all a rush—binge on the weekend kind of stuff—but when we get into our early twenties we take different paths. Some of us give it up completely, save for the odd social occasion, but for others it's a crutch, a reset button, a necessity. I fall into the latter category. These days I need to drink at home in order to feel relaxed enough to go out and drink even more. Life feels too mundane without a constant high. Alcohol in the evening, caffeine in the morning. It's a vicious cycle, but one I'm reluctant to give up.

I finish the bottle and debate cracking open another when the Phoenix lets me know that Velvet Crush are playing at the Middle East tonight. They're a tight combo from Providence and I dig their melodic pop sounds. It's been awhile since I've seen a good concert. I decide to be social.

I had only been to Boston once before on a brief trip to visit Paul, so it feels a little surreal that I'm actually living here now. Yesterday I took the subway—the T as they call it here—to the city center to have a walk around. Parts of Boston look very European and at times I felt like I was back on the continent, until I came across the locals. I wished I had my Discman with me to drown out the sounds of honking cars and the crowd of angry pale men in suits.

I immediately feel at home in the club. It's a strange little venue. One has to walk through a cozy Middle Eastern restaurant (hence the club name) to a door in back to get inside. It's a small, relatively clean room with a good sound system and friendly vibe. There are maybe thirty people in attendance, making it feel more like a private party than a proper concert. I catch the last few songs from the opening band, a mod-inspired trio called the Pills. When they started lugging their equipment offstage, I go to the bar to buy a beer. Everyone around me is drinking Rolling Rock, apparently the beverage of choice for the in-crowd here. I opt for a Guinness, which is poured in the proper Irish fashion, making me wonder if the bartender is one of the many Irish expats who have made their way to this city. The verdict is still out on Boston, but I'm reassured to know that, if nothing else, I can at least track down a good pint. Standing to my right is a pale pretty girl with short, meticulously messy, dark brown hair. A Winona Ryder type. She's wearing jeans, a black turtleneck, and a stylish leather jacket. Her lipstick is bright red and there's a small silver hooped earring pierced through her right eyebrow. Everything about her screams trouble and high maintenance, but her beautiful smile and blue-green eyes draw me in like the proverbial moth to flame.

"So are you going to see Blur when they come to Avalon next month?" she asks a guy standing to her right.

"For sure," he says. He's a skinny mod kid who looks like Danny from Supergrass. He hiccups and continues, "They're my favorite band at the moment along with Pulp."

"Whipping Boy are better," I say, surprised that I've barged into their conversation. I'm usually reserved with strangers, but this girl is getting to me.

"Who are they?" she asks. "Are they English? I've never

heard of them." She looks at me like I'm the most interesting guy in the room even though we've just met.

"They're Irish," I say, trying to control my nerves, wishing I were a little more drunk and at ease. "If you're into bands like Joy Division and Echo and the Bunnymen, you'll love them."

"I'd probably like them then. I love everything from across the pond."

Danny joins some friends near the stage, leaving me alone with little miss heartbreaker.

"So how do you know out about Whipping Boy?" she asks. "Do you read a lot of magazines? I write for the Harvard Crimson and read every English magazine I can get my hands on."

She's quite animated. The mention of a band she hasn't heard of has put her into full Nancy Drew mode, or maybe Harvard students just don't like it when outsiders know things they don't.

"I lived in Ireland for a long time," I say. "I saw them play a few times." I try to compose myself so I can go on to tell her how great *Heartworm* is without sounding like a nerdy fanboy, but we're rudely interrupted by a young Aryan gent who looks like he could be a rower or rugby player.

"Come on, Emily," he says in an aggressive tone. "Lawrence and Mackie are here. They want to say hi to you."

He puts his hand on her shoulder and steers her in the direction of his friends, like he's maneuvering a shopping cart. They walk away, hand in hand. Emily turns one last time and winks at me. Her switchblade smile cuts straight through my heart.

I have a tough time focusing on Velvet Crush, preoccupied by an entirely different crush, trying my hardest to lock eyes with Emily one last time. She and her friends leave after a few songs and my pulse finally drops. Velvet Crush are great, ripping through a stellar set that mixes in old favorites from the first album with some new tunes, including "This Life is Killing Me," possibly their best song to date. The drummer Ric is a real character, getting up from behind his kit after every song to tell corny jokes to the crowd. Maybe Boston won't be so bad after all, I think.

I'm sadly mistaken.

On my walk home, I encounter three Hispanic teens on Central Avenue. They're hanging out at a crosswalk with a young girl, who looks maybe fourteen at best. I notice the bottle of wine being passed around. I avoid eye contact, but one of them approaches me anyway. A short, shifty guy with a gold tooth who smells like wine, vomit, and cheap cologne. He asks if I have any cash. I reach into my pocket and hand him three singles.

"Sorry, man, that's all I have," I say.

I walk away. They follow me despite the girl's pleas to "leave him alone." I consider running—I'm pretty sure I can outleg them—but I stick to walking at a brisk pace, not wanting them to sniff out panic.

Gold Tooth and one of his compadres, a chubby kid in an oversized down jacket, which makes him look like the Michelin Man, catch up to me.

"Don't disrespect me, bro," says Gold Tooth. "You dissin' me."

"What do you mean?" I ask. "That's all the cash I have."

"Ain't that," says Gold Tooth. "You walk away like you're better than us."

"Just heading home," I say. "I don't want any trouble."

Gold Tooth punches me in the face. I instinctively tuck my head into my elbows and feel another blow to the back of my head. Suddenly, I'm on the ground in a fetal position, desperately plotting an exit strategy. The girl starts screaming.

"Leave him alone," she pleads.

"Shut up, bitch," says the third assailant. He kicks me in the ribs. Gold Tooth follows suit with a few football kicks of his own. Michelin Man holds back the girl, who is now screaming at the top of her lungs. After a few minutes of painful kicks to the guts and ribs, plus another blow to my head, I'm saved by a townie with a huge beer gut. He appears out of somewhere clutching a baseball bat. He looks like an off-duty prison guard or cop, which is enough to scare off the posse.

"That's right, go back to where you came from you fucking wetbacks," he yells.

"You okay, chief?" he asks after my assailants flee.

I nod, too winded to even speak, and flash him a thumbs up sign.

"Anytime. You know, kid, Central Avenue ain't the safest stretch for walking after dark."

"Noted," I gasp.

"Be careful, chief. Boston can be a mean town."

When I get home I wash the blood off my face and take

a long, deep look into the mirror. I have a decent-sized shiner and my ribs are severely bruised. I should probably see a doctor. I go to the kitchen and pop a Benadryl, washing it down with a large gulp of wine. The combination of alcohol and antihistamine have given me lucid dreams in the past. Maybe if I'm lucky I'll visit Claire in my sleep and she'll wish me happy birthday, or maybe Emily will appear in her place, offering a new beginning. I start sobbing like a baby. Loneliness is a gun.

When We Were Young

In March I take a train to New York to visit my old friend Johnny. We're going to see Oasis at the Paramount. The last time I saw them in Dublin they weren't so great. The singer, Liam Gallagher, was annoying, pouting like a prima donna during his brother Noel's guitar solos. At one point I thought Noel was going to punch him. The highlight of the evening was when a drunk guy next to me gave Liam the thumbs down sign. Liam stuck his thumb up in response as if to say, "You've got me wrong, man. I'm a fookin' rock 'n' roll star." After the guy flashed the thumbs down sign again, Liam signaled for him to come up on stage. The guy tried to confront Liam but was promptly escorted away by security.

I arrive during rush hour. Johnny greets me at Penn Station. He was my best friend at Essex. We bonded instantly, the two of us going to pubs, clubs, and gigs, soaking in the vibrant English music scene. Johnny the musician, me the aspiring scribe. After leaving university, Johnny put his energy into his band, Competition Orange. They had a decent run, releasing several acclaimed indie records in the late eighties that appealed to people who rated bands like the Jesus and Mary Chain and Ultra Vivid Scene. But their fate took a nose dive when they signed to a major. By then the Manchester sound was all the rage, and the new label bullied Competition Orange into compromising their sound. Some Hollywood producer neutered everything. I remember a frustrated Johnny telling me how the Happy Mondays' "Loose Fit" was played on loop as a motivation tool. Even though the band got decent press and had their video played a few times on *120 Minutes*, that wasn't enough for the label, who dropped them when it became clear they wouldn't recoup their debt.

Johnny was a fashionable mod back then, and still is. Today he's wearing a tailored black suit. I made an effort to look reasonably nice for my visit, sporting Chelsea boots, brown cords, and a long sleeve black T-shirt underneath my leather jacket, but I feel like a slob next to Johnny. I always do.

I compliment him, but he brushes it off, sounding almost apologetic.

"I just got off of work. Have to look good for the man. I need to get home and change into something more casual."

"I like the look," I say. "You're the true Modfather. Fuck Paul Weller."

"Careful, there," he teases when I poke fun at his idol. "You're looking good, too, Drew. It's been way too long."

We take a cab to the lower east side where Johnny lives with roommates. I comment that the neighborhood looks more gentrified than the last time I was in New York in '89, but it's still scary. Johnny says not to worry—that Thurston Moore and Kim Gordon from Sonic Youth live a few blocks from here.

Johnny changes into a Ben Sherman dress shirt and a parka and we head out to the Kiev restaurant. I'm half-Ukrainian, but know little about my homeland. I do love the food though. Johnny says there are a lot of cute waitresses who are straight off the boat.

We knock back several beers apiece as we plow through

borscht and Ukrainian dumplings, called varenyky. The young blonde server sneaks us refills, telling us that we look too skinny.

"So damn, Drew, it's good to see you. I feel like we're back in Colchester again, only this time with good Ukrainian food and not that crappy English grub."

"I know what you mean. I still think about the old days all the time. Do you remember how I was all set to move to New York and be your roommate?"

"Yeah."

"But then I met Claire."

He doesn't say anything. There isn't much to say.

"Shit, I didn't mean to bum you out," I say. "Sometimes I just can't let go. I've been questioning everything lately."

"I hear you, man. I've had some good times, but that optimism and lust for life I felt back then has definitely waned."

We cab it to a pub within walking distance of the concert venue, where we meet up with my boss at Spin, Nick Danger. I met Nick during my Essex year, too. Back then I was a music critic for my college newspaper in Michigan, desperate to advance my career. Nick, who was a star writer for Melody Maker, became a mentor of sorts. One day I decided to track him down at his London office and we became friends, bonding that evening over drinks, a Primal Scream concert, and a post-concert bender with Alan McGee, Bobby Gillespie, and others in the Creation entourage.

Nick's doing well. He recently married an attorney, who doesn't seem to mind his rock 'n' roll lifestyle. Nick used to be a twee indie kid, but now reminds me more of Dave, no doubt buying his clothes wherever music biz guys with large bank accounts shop. He opens a tab, handing over an American Express card to the bartender, telling me and Johnny that drinks are on him. We start with shots of Jameson.

"To Drew leaving Ireland behind," says Nick.

"Good fucking riddance," says Johnny.

We're in an Irish pub and a few of the punters there throw us dirty looks. I don't care. I'm feeling loose. We leave the bar area and find an open booth. There's a good hour or two to kill before Oasis come on. Nick mentions that he can get us backstage. Johnny says he doesn't like Oasis but is dying to see what the fuss is about.

"A band like Oasis wouldn't have gotten a second look in the eighties," says Johnny. "You and Drew need to raise the bar and write about music that matters."

"Fucking A," I say. "I'll drink to that."

I take a large gulp of Guinness and say, "I don't mind Oasis, but they don't hold a candle to the Jesus and Mary Chain, Smiths, or Stone Roses. You need to let me do an article about Whipping Boy, Nick. Have you heard *Heartworm* yet? Christ, it's amazing."

"I love that record," says Nick, "but the band is far too obscure for a feature. My friend Rob at Alternative Press might be able to help you out. I'll give you his info. They're much more cutting edge than Spin will ever be. I'd love to work for them, but that would mean living in Cleveland."

We're suitably sloshed when we arrive at the venue. The gig is a bit of a blur. We get there just as the opening act has finished. Liam Gallagher walks onstage with ex-Verve singer Richard Ashcroft and mumbles something to the crowd before Richard bangs out a few acoustic numbers that sound all grown-up and mainstream, songs that might appeal to Sting's fans. Finally, Oasis appear and they have the crowd eating putty out of their hands. It's like the Bay City Rollers with feedback, obligatory audience sing-a-longs and all that jazz.

When it's over we go backstage. It's sad seeing Ashcroft in this element. The Verve were on fire last year, releasing one of the best albums of the decade, *A Northern Soul*, before their sudden, unexpected breakup. The man has the most musical talent in the room, but now seems content to be a bland adult contemporary singer. He even looks the part. He's got trendy cropped hair and is wearing a green Lacoste shirt, a far cry from the freaky 'Mad Richard' days when he sported wild shoulder length locks and told journalists it was only a matter of time before people would literally be able to fly.

Johnny corners Liam and tells him that "Supersonic" sounds like the Happy Mondays' "Kinky Afro Groove," a comparison Liam probably doesn't want to hear.

"In fact, you could almost call it 'Supersonic Afro Groove,'" Johnny says.

Liam turns red and flails his arms, like he's some sort of thug toddler, before poking Johnny in the chest. "You're wasting my time, man. You're wasting my time," he says.

Johnny and I laugh as Liam walks away. Nick throws us a dirty look as if we're two kids misbehaving at the adult table. We run into brother Noel on the way out. I tell him that I know Dave—a test to see if Dave was bullshitting to me that night at the Columbia. Noel icily responds that

Dave is a fookin' smackhead, always hanging out with Donna Matthews from Elastica and her lot.

Johnny and I bolt. We go to a dive bar that, according to Johnny, has the best jukebox in the world. Tonight there's a DJ, Jack Rabid from acclaimed fanzine The Big Takeover. The place stinks of black mold and cigarettes. Appropriately, "Sonic Reducer" greets us at the door as we maneuver our way to the bar.

We find two stools near the DJ booth and Johnny orders some Rolling Rocks. I'm starting to feel wrecked, but don't want the evening to end.

"I miss the time we spent together at Essex," I say for about the tenth time. "I think about those days all the time."

"I do, too, man," says Johnny. "I don't think I would have continued with the band if I didn't have you to inspire me. You stuck to your guns and made it as writer, man."

"I wouldn't say I made it, but I appreciate what you're saying. You inspired me, too, man. You were on MTV. That's something to drink to."

We clink bottles.

"I'm scared to move on," I say. "Life was a lot easier then. I don't know how to grow up and live with myself. How do you do it? You're still cool, Johnny. You didn't become a fucking douche." I'm starting to slur.

Johnny laughs. "You think I'm cool? I'd throw away my fucking job in a second if I could get the band back together. Someday I'm going to get married and have a kid or two, but, man, I'm still young, aren't I. Let's worry about this shit if we're still drinking in this place ten years from now."

"Agreed."

At this point, "When We Were Young" booms through the speakers. It's the new single from *Heartworm*, an infectiously catchy ode to sex, drugs, rock 'n' roll, and youth. I'm thrilled that Jack knows Whipping Boy. The song packs more punch in three minutes than a flawless coming-of-age film like *Quadrophenia* does in two hours. One line in particular resonates with me: "The first time that you loved you had all your life to give." Even in my blackest moods I know I'll fall in love again, but I also know I won't be able to surrender as willingly as I did with Claire. And that makes me sad.

Later, Jack plays "Chinese Rocks."

I order some shots.

"To Johnny Fucking Thunders," I say.

"To Johnny Fucking Thunders," says Johnny.

Some barely legal punk girls invite us to dance. You know the type. Ripped fishnets, manic panic hair color, strategic piercings in all the right (and wrong) places. "Chinese Rocks" fades into the Stones' "Rocks Off." I can't remember the last time I felt a need to be reckless. Probably the year I spent in England with Johnny. When we were young. Johnny and I dance a few numbers with the girls before sneaking out when it's clear that one of them has taken a strong liking to him.

"She's kind of hot in a sleazy way," he says, "but I don't want to wake up to an empty apartment and a disease."

"But, don't you want to get your Chinese Rocks off?"

Johnny laughs. We hail a taxi and annoy the cabbie by singing a medley composed of excerpts from the two songs: "I'm living on a Chinese rock because the sunshine bores the daylights out of me."

Red Dragon

A few days after returning from New York I go for a walk on an unseasonably warm evening. I find myself outside a dive Chinese joint somewhere between Central and Harvard Square. The décor looks like it hasn't changed much since the seventies, the flickering red neon sign above about to blow its last wad. I go inside. It's a small joint, furnished with a long bar, several tables, and a couple of black leather booths in the back. The red light gives the place a dreamlike quality, as if I've stepped into a David Lynch film set.

I take a seat at the bar. The bartender, an oriental guy with long black hair and a Fu Manchu mustache, asks what I want to drink.

"Just a beer," I say.

"Tsingtao, okay?"

"Sure."

"Make it a Double Happiness," says a voice to my right. "And another for me."

I look over and lock eyes with a tall pale man in a dark suit.

"What's a Double Happiness?" I ask.

"A shot of whiskey washed down with Tsingtao."

"Thanks, man. I'm Drew," I say, reaching out my hand.

"I'm Loren. So what brings you here? No one comes to the Red Dragon to get happy. What are we drinking to?"

"Dead friends and dead ends."

"To better days," says Loren.

We clink glasses and knock back our shots. Loren looks a little older than me, probably mid-thirties. He has dark brown hair, worn long in front but tight and conservative on the back and sides. He looks a little like me. I wonder if he's my doppelganger. I also wonder why he's hanging out in a dive like this, decked out in such an elegant suit.

"That's Jethro," says Loren, pointing to the barman who's left us to rinse glasses. "He doesn't say much, but he's a righteous dude."

"Jethro's a cool name," I say.

"From what he's told me, his parents liked westerns. They wanted to give him a cowboy name. Jethro Chang is a damn good cowboy name if you ask me."

"He looks like he could be a character in a Tarantino movie," I say.

"You like Tarantino?"

"Depends on the flick. *Reservoir Dogs*, yes. *Pulp Fiction*, not so much."

"What's wrong with *Pulp Fiction*?"

"I hate Travolta. I can't get past *Saturday Night Fever*. That whole bit at the end about just wanting to strut is an all-time low in cinema history."

Loren laughs. "You're all right with me, Drew. I'm with

you on *Reservoir Dogs*. And *True Romance*. That flick is fierce."

When we finish our drinks, I order another round and venture over to the jukebox. The music seems to have been selected with heartache in mind; nothing but bluesy RnB, sad country and western, and damaged rock 'n' roll. I feed some bills into the machine and make my selections. Isaac Hayes "Walk On By," Kristofferson "Sunday Morning Coming Down," Rolling Stones "Monkey Man," and Womack "Across 110th Street."

I go to the bathroom and splash some water on my face. Even though it's night time, I'm overheating. The winter here was cold and miserable and now, suddenly, it feels like full on summer. I miss the bland Irish climate. I look into the mirror. My long sleeve black T-shirt is clinging to my skin. I feel too skinny like I did when I was a competitive runner in high school. I look unhealthy, like an NME heroin chic poster boy.

I return to the bar and Loren asks if I'm okay.

"Yeah, man, I'm good. Just not used to this heat. I feel all sweaty and gross."

"You don't look it, man. You're very rock 'n' roll. You've got that Rolling Stones Altamont thing going on. Are you in a band?"

"No, closest I've come is writing about it."

"Who do you write for?" he asks.

"I wrote for Hot Press when I lived in Ireland and I've freelanced for Spin on and off for years."

"Nice. Milk it while you can. Careers are overrated. I used

to be into music when I was young. Saw the Sex Pistols in Tulsa on their first U.S. tour, even bought Sid a beer. Lone Star, if I recall correctly. I still keep up with the magazines, but don't go to gigs much anymore."

"Christ, I thought you were closer to my age. I was in junior high school when the Sex Pistols came to America."

"I'm older than I look, I guess," says Loren. "I just turned forty."

"Well, you look good man. What do you do for work?"

"I'm an investment banker."

"That's impressive. I don't have the fortitude to do anything like that."

"I just fell into it," he says. "I'm good at helping rich people get richer. Disgusting isn't it?"

"Have you always worked in finance?"

"Hell, no. I've done all kinds of shit. I dropped out of college and worked retail for a long time, mainly record stores. I moved out here for a chick, but when that didn't work out I decided to stay. I was working an admin job at Harvard and finished my degree at the extension school. I just fell into banking and seem to be good at it. I keep getting promoted without trying and keep drinking to forget that I'm good at my job."

"Man, I'm jealous you saw the Sex Pistols," I say, steering the conversation back to a more pleasant topic. "Who else did you see back in the day?"

"Gang of Four were really awesome and I got to see Mötorhead, too. That was super cool. My buddy worked for the local weekly and we got to interview Lemmy at a strip club. It was a trip."

"Nice."

"Sure was. I miss those days. I use to be so passionate about music, especially going to gigs. It's like I hit thirty and stopped wanting to get any kicks."

"I think everyone I know is waiting for that to happen to me, but I feel like I've been stuck at twenty-one forever. I'm thirty-one and I've never really done anything grown-up except endure toxic relationships."

"That's why I never succumb to a woman's spell," says Loren. "I just stay with chicks until they get sick of me and move on to the next one. The path of least resistance."

"You've never been in love?" I ask.

"A few times when I was young and dumb, I guess. Not anymore. If you can't find a young chick who wants a casual arrangement, high-class call girls are the way to go. They're a much better investment than the dating scene. You don't have to buy them dinner and they'll leave when you tell them to. It's a simple transaction."

"You get hookers?" I ask in disbelief. I can't tell if he's fucking with me, but Loren maintains his poker face, talking about women in the same way I imagine he conducts his business deals.

"Don't knock it if you haven't tried it, brother. I'm not talking about the street walker variety, just the stone foxes you can hire from a service. I have a connection if you're interested."

"I'll pass for now," I say with a smile.

"So what brings you to Boston?" asks Loren.

I tell Loren how I met Claire when I was a student at Essex. Instead of coming home when I was supposed to, I moved to Ireland to be with her. We bummed around for a year, went back to Michigan so I could finish my degree, and then returned to Ireland again when Claire got accepted into a Ph.D. program at Trinity College. I don't tell Loren how things ended, just that my brother bailed me out and gave me a place to stay.

"So where are you living?" asks Loren.

I give him a swank address off Memorial Drive.

"Damn, brother. Enjoy it while you can."

"For sure. My digs are the only thing that feels good in my life right now."

I have no idea what time it is now. It feels like permanent midnight inside the Red Dragon, like we're in limbo. No one has come into the bar since I arrived, but Jethro doesn't seem concerned. He's packing a bowl.

"You guys wanna toke?" he asks.

He looks happy but I can tell that Jethro's the kind of guy you don't want to cross. The kind who might buy you a drink one minute and slit your throat the next. Maybe it's the mustache, but he scares me.

"Sure," I say.

"Sure, man," says Loren.

Loren takes a long hit and passes the pipe to me. I take a hit just as "I Got the Blues" kicks in.

"Fuck," I say. "I didn't notice *Sticky Fingers* was on the jukebox. Did you put that on?"

"Damn straight," says Loren. "Best album ever, especially the last four songs on Side Two. I love bumming out to this record at home with whiskey or wine."

I'm not sure why Loren seems so sad. He has a high-paying job, and he's tall and good-looking. He should be soaking in trim. "Sister Morphine" is on now, the ultimate coming-down ballad. I love Marianne Faithfull's rendition too (she co-wrote the song), but there's something about Jagger's delivery and Keith Richards' fucked-up guitar tones that makes this the definitive take.

Reading my mind, Loren asks if I like Marianne Faithfull. I admit to only knowing "Sister Morphine" and another Stones song she covered, "As Tears Go By."

"Gotta check her out, brother," he says as Mick announces that in the morning he'll be dead. "She acted, too. If you ever get to see the Kenneth Anger flick *Lucifer Rising*, check it out. It's a mind fuck."

"Dead Flowers" is on now and Loren, who has seemed relatively soft spoken thus far, becomes quite animated. "Do you dig Townes Van Zandt?"

"I don't know him," I say.

"Dude, you have to check him out. He has a downbeat country vibe. He covered 'Dead Flowers.' His version gives me the fucking chills." Loren puts emphasis on the curse word. "But that just might be me, dude. I grew up in Tulsa—my dad is an oil man—I have a soft spot for all that depressing cowboy shit."

We take another hit and that's all I remember.

Ghost of Elvis

I wake up on the futon at home, covered in sweat, the bed sheet clinging to me, the chorus from the Whipping Boy song "Tripped" ringing in my ears. "She tripped, she tripped. She had nothing left to give." I need to piss. I get up and nearly crush a CD case on the living room floor. It's *Heartworm*. I must have fallen asleep listening to it. I take care of business and get back into bed, burying myself underneath the covers. Suddenly, I'm cold. I think about Claire, how her mother's death did her head in. We had been going through a rough patch already, but Ann's passing a year and a half ago put Claire over the edge. She was never the same. A doctor put her on meds to ease the nerves, but nothing seemed to shake her depression. She dropped out of school. She became borderline anorexic. I could barely get her to eat anything other than cans of sweet corn. In desperation, one of Claire's girlfriends took her to a spiritual healing center in Sandymount. That's where she met her Gaelic shaman Sean.

Sean was a twelve stepper. A former junkie who found new age religion. He was old—pushing forty—and looked it with his weather-beaten face and long gray ponytail. He told Claire that crystals healed his addiction. She became convinced he was her savior. It sinks in that I don't even know where Claire lives anymore. I recently tried phoning her at the shop she worked at in Glastonbury. A dopey West Country girl answered my call and told me Claire wasn't in. She took a message. It was never returned. I tried again a few weeks later and the same girl informed me that Claire didn't work there anymore, something about her and Sean moving to Bath. No, she didn't have a forwarding address. I debated whether or not to phone Gordon, Claire's father. I assumed he knew. If he didn't, I didn't want to be the one to tell him. I briefly indulged in a West Country "Kentucky Rain" fantasy where I would scour English towns in search of my true love. Just like Elvis.

I remember a conversation I had about the King with Paul from Whipping Boy. It was just after Ann died. I had gone to see Into Paradise at the Rock Garden and ran into him there. He asked how I was doing. I told him I had just come back from the funeral in Belfast. He bought me a drink. The support act wasn't very good so we just sat at the bar and talked. I didn't know Paul too well back then. Prior to that, the only time we talked was during the Hot Press interview and brief chats at various concerts. We ended up bonding that evening. He told me that his dad had died when he was seventeen and that he knew what Claire was going through. I told him about my childhood best friend, PJ, who had died in a drunken car wreck and how I still thought about him a lot. I said that in dark times rock 'n' roll was my best friend.

"Rock 'n' roll saved my life, too," said Paul. "After my father died, I took refuge in music. Playing my guitar as loud as I could kept me sane. I wanted to be like Will Sergeant from Echo and the Bunnymen."

"You and me, both. Only I can't play music, so I write about it. The Bunnymen are one of my all-time favorite bands. All the girls I knew back then had massive crushes on Ian, but I loved Will, too. He looked really cool, like Sterling Morrison or something."

"I saw them play in '84 and after that, nothing else mattered," said Paul.

At this point the opening act finished their set and the house stereo kicked in with an obnoxiously loud live U2 track where Bono segues into Elvis' "Can't Help Falling in Love."

"I used to like U2," I said, "but this is plain embarrassing."

"No argument from me," said Paul. "Bono's a wanker. Do you like Elvis?"

"I do, but funny enough, it's the later period that resonates with me most, like 'In The Ghetto,' 'Kentucky Rain,' and 'Suspicious Minds.'"

"'Suspicious Minds' would be a great song to cover," said Paul.

"Maybe you'll get the chance to someday. I'm sure you'd do a fantastic version. There's something really honest and vulnerable about those Memphis recordings."

"That's something we're hoping to capture on the new record," said Paul. "Honesty and vulnerability. *Submarine* is okay, but it's too generic. The next one is going to be much better."

Paul went on to tell me how Whipping Boy had just signed to Columbia Records and were about to start recording at Windmill Lane Studios. Though famous because of its association with the early U2 albums, it's a non-descript building save for the walls caked in moronic graffiti by fans from all over the world. Locals know it as the house that Bono built, or as Henry Rollins calls it, the mecca for shitheads. Nevertheless, Paul was excited because they were going to work with Warne Livesey, the man who produced the House of Love's *Babe Rainbow*, a record that I also rated.

"So what are your new songs like?" I asked.

Paul paused and seemed lost for words until he finally said, "Let's just say that it will be unlike any other Irish record around. You know that Velvet Underground live album *1969*? There's a passage on the inside sleeve, like an essay, that talks about 'Heroin' being played in fifty years' time, and children studying it in school. I don't want to sound that pretentious, but I'd like to think that our new record will mean something to at least a few individuals—people like you and me—who will later say it was part of their growing up."

At this point Into Paradise took the stage and Paul and I worked our way to the front. Into Paradise were once a great Irish hope. Their stunning 1990 debut *Under The Water*, released on Dublin expat Keith Cullen's trendy London-based imprint Setanta Records, garnered enough critical acclaim that the band signed a major label distribution deal with Chrysalis. That record and the even darker follow up *Churchtown* were glorious slabs of moody postpunk in a similar vein to legends like Joy Division, the Chameleons, and the Sound. Adrian Borland even produced some of the early records. In an ideal world Into Paradise would have been massive, but like the vast majority of major label signees, the stars didn't align. They remained a beloved cult band with beloved cult band sales figures, and Chrysalis abruptly dropped them. The gig Paul and I witnessed turned out to be one of their last.

I didn't know the singer Dave Long too well, but I could sense his frustration. I remembered a candid piece in the Irish Times from the year before when Dave talked about his group's then new album *For No One*. He had high hopes for the single "Move Over," a song as epic and magical as the best U2 anthems like "Bad" and "The Unforgettable Fire." Long said something to the effect that if the song didn't become a hit, he didn't know what else to do because he couldn't top that.

The Rock Garden gig was sparsely attended, but everyone there seemed to know the band and love their music. It was an intimate atmosphere, a celebration of sorts; in retrospect, a wake. Paul was standing with me near the front, a huge smile on his face. I felt like I was witnessing a changing of the guard. Whipping Boy were about to begin their major label career while some ten feet away from us stood the once mighty Into Paradise. I could see the parallels with my own life. Paul represented the younger me from a decade ago, about to board a flight to London, idealistic and green, head full of dreams about becoming a famous rock critic. Dave was the current me who had his moment in the sun and now realized that the music life wasn't all that it was cracked up to be. There's nothing in life as exhilarating and heartbreaking as rock 'n' roll.

Into Paradise's set was incredible. The band focused on newer material with a few old classics thrown in for good measure. While less animated than a lot of singers—no strutting, voguing, or mic stand acrobatics—Dave can be an imposing force on stage. He's a large man with a shock of wavy jet black hair who lets his words and statuesque presence do all the talking. At an Into Paradise performance you get the feeling that Dave lives every word of the romantic heartbreak that pours out of his songs. That evening was a classic case of killing me softly as I listened to Dave's lyrics and thought about my dying marriage. On "Sister" Dave sang, "Sleep comes down and kills the bad dreams," and I yearned for some kind of release. Near the end of the set the band played a blistering version of "Like a Hurricane," my favorite Neil Young song. Hours later I woke up in bed, Claire sound asleep beside me, Neil's words and the echoes from the amplifiers ringing in my head: "I want to love you but I'm getting blown away." Claire lay inches from me, but it felt like we were a million miles apart.

The Honeymoon is Over

It's early April and I'm flying to London. Nick came through and connected me with Rob Cherry, the editor-in-chief of Alternative Press magazine. Rob was excited about my pitch—he digs Whipping Boy—and even offered me two hundred dollars for the assignment. I didn't tell him that I would have done it for free. Instead of scheduling a standard phone interview, I decide to max out a credit card and do this one in person. Whipping Boy aren't coming to America, having chosen to open for Lou Reed in Europe instead of supporting dire industrial act, Stabbing Westward, in the States. The chance to witness the London show and meet Lou is too good to pass up, bills be damned.

Heartworm is spinning on my Discman and I've gone through several miniature bottles of airplane red, not the best cocktail for inducing happiness, but I find Fearghal's words therapeutic. They're forcing me to unlock painful memories buried deep in my psyche. The album has become an ally of sorts, my shrink.

"The Honeymoon is Over" is spinning now, a doomed ballad reminiscent of Nick Cave at his finest. Fearghal sings, "The honeymoon is over and you're still with me," and I'm immediately transported to the early stages of my relationship with Claire. I can pinpoint when it all went wrong and wonder why we bothered to keep trying. Most relationships are diseased compromises. Some people bail when the spark is gone, hoping to rekindle the fire with someone else, while others suffer in silence, dying slow deaths, too stubborn to admit defeat.

Our first year together was the best. Claire and I were working part-time at her uncle's pub in Dublin, living rent free in a beautiful gate lodge in Killiney, situated on her uncle's property. We didn't have much and didn't seem to need it. Once a week we would go to Bewley's on Grafton Street and order an overpriced tea service with scones and assorted jams. That was our only vice. Other nights we'd take a long walk on the picturesque Killiney Road, ending up at the Dalkey Island Hotel for a quiet pint or two. Then Claire and my parents talked me into finishing school in Michigan.

"It's only a year, and it will give you more career options," Claire said. She was too cute to say no to back then, so I succumbed.

Going back to Ann Arbor after two years abroad felt like returning home from 'Nam. As soon as the plane landed, I was jonesing to get back across the pond. I felt like Walken in *The Deer Hunter*, fixing for a game of Russian roulette. Just before classes started, we saw an amazing triple bill, consisting of Echo and the Bunnymen, New Order, and Gene Loves Jezebel, at a goofy outdoor venue called Pine Knob, located in the wilderness halfway between Detroit and Flint. The music was great, but the atmosphere made me sad, damn near suicidal. Before the show, I noticed some stoners in the parking lot drinking beer, passing around a joint, listening to the Cult. They were blasting out the ballad "Revolution" and it may as well have been something trite like "American Pie." The kids were okay, but the atmosphere got to me. Everything felt so 'American,' so alien, and it made me homesick for a place I barely knew.

Claire took to America though. She worked at Urban Outfitters while I finished my degree. I'm pretty sure every remotely cool guy in Ann Arbor had a massive crush on her. Claire liked being the center of attention. She stood out with her unique accent and impeccable fashion sense, so our planned one year in Michigan somehow morphed into three. Eventually, Claire got tired of working retail and decided to go back to school. In retrospect, I should have known better; a woman going back to school can be a kiss of death to even the strongest relationship. I had been working at a record store and freelancing for Spin, and while I wasn't unhappy, I jumped at the opportunity to return to Ireland, even promising to get a real job. During the Christmas holiday Claire and I got married in Belfast at a small civil ceremony in a courthouse, attended by family and a few close friends.

Rock 'n' roll's sharp, unforgiving claws were still buried deep in my skin. I started writing for Hot Press again, continued to take assignments for Spin, and had more late nights than I should have had working a nine-to-five job. Claire and I began to drift apart. She took her studies seriously. Like my father, her dad was a professor. We laughed about this when we first met, but the joke wasn't so funny when it became clear that she wanted a lifestyle I wasn't on board with.

This made her insecure, often mean. She frowned on me having a social life, constantly telling me that if I really loved her, I wouldn't need anyone or anything else. While it was okay for her to socialize with classmates, she thought my passion for music was downright pathetic. On more than one occasion she told me I had become a sad, old rock 'n' roller. Even my office job wasn't good enough for her. She thought I wasn't making enough money working for a non-profit and became convinced that I should get a job in finance. At one point she dragged me out to buy a set of wicker furniture, convinced that having a grown up flat would somehow transform me into the young professional of her dreams.

In the evenings I was expected to be at her beck and call, ready to make tea at a moment's notice when she needed a study break. If I left the flat to see a gig, there'd be hell to pay. I'd get the cold treatment for days on end. Then her mom died. The final nail in the coffin.

Portholes for Bono

The Whipping Boy concert is at Shepherd's Bush Empire in West London, the Who's old stomping grounds. I arrive early for the interview and the door guy is kind enough to give me a quick tour of the venue. It's a massive yet intimate theater with a capacity of two thousand, containing two tiers of balconies, complete with plush red velvet seats. I'm getting goose bumps imagining how great Whipping Boy are going to sound.

When I go backstage, the guys are happy and surprised to see me.

"Drew, bloody hell. Didn't realize it was you who was doing this interview," says Paul. "We just knew it was for some American magazine."

"What magazine?" asks the singer Fearghal. He looks like a true rock 'n' roll god tonight, sporting a gold dress shirt and black leather trousers. The other guys are dressed in jeans and dark T-shirts.

"Alternative Press," I say, retrieving the latest issue from my backpack, featuring the Flaming Lips on the front cover.

"Will we be on the cover?" asks bass player Myles, who's never been shy. "We just blew Ride off the stage in Dublin. You would have loved it."

"Wish I could have seen it," I say. "I miss Dublin. I hope you guys can come to America though I would have chosen Lou Reed over Stabbing Westward, too."

"Exactly, mate," says Fearghal.

He seems relaxed. I don't know Fearghal and the drummer Colm so well. I've always been friendly with Paul, and, by default, Myles. The two grew up together and are close. They're an interesting combo. Paul is soft spoken and shy until you get to know him, while Myles can be brash and cocky. The only time I've talked to Fearghal is when I interviewed him and Paul for Hot Press. I was nervous before that interview, having heard stories about Fearghal's drunken outbursts. Expecting the worst, I was pleasantly surprised at how polite and shy he was. A few months later I approached Fearghal after a particularly intense performance—the gig where he charged into the guy in the audience—to tell him how much I enjoyed the show. Fearghal was quite animated, yelling at a punter who had heckled him earlier. He barely recognized me, so I slipped away, not wanted to upset him further.

This time I'm doing the interview with Paul, Myles, and Fearghal. Colm and a Dublin lad named Killian, who will be playing guitar and keyboards with the group on this tour, leave the room, each of them liberating a bottle of Stella from the ice bucket on the floor. Everyone is in fantastic spirits. I tell them how much I love the record, how it's holding me hostage. I pry them about the genesis of their masterpiece.

Paul is the first to speak. "After *Submarine* we retired to a tiny dingy rehearsal room where we drew a real strength and defiance out of the whole label collapse. If felt very much like us against the world. We wrote a lot of *Heartworm* there and just started demoing material."

"One of the engineers passed on a tape with 'We Don't

Need Nobody Else' to someone he knew at Columbia," says Myles, who jumps in, excited to relive the memory.

I remind Paul how he told me that it would be unlike any Irish record around.

He laughs and says, "And it is, isn't it?"

I smile.

"Everyone in Dublin still wants to be like R.E.M. and U2," says Fearghal. "We weren't listening to trendy indie music when we were making *Heartworm*. This came from the heart."

The three of them toss around names like Nick Cave, Leonard Cohen, Velvet Underground, Joy Division, and Paul's beloved Bunnymen.

Paul, who co-wrote the music with Myles says, "I have never been a fan of music top heavy on screeching guitar solos and that real fast two hundred notes a second guitar work. It just never held any fascination for me. I've always preferred more textural playing, which creates a mood. I'm a huge fan of Will Sergeant, particularly the early material, and I was influenced by the Kitchens of Distinction's guitar sound."

"What was it like recording with Warne Livesey?" I ask. "I love the orchestrated vibe he captured on *Heartworm*."

"Warne was great," says Paul. "He's a chill guy."

"We liked him. We bought him a Mr. Noisy T-shirt when we finished recording," laughs Myles.

"We did drive him a bit mad at times," says Fearghal. "We were always referring to the demos as a point of reference, but he took it well."

"He really helped us finesse our sound," says Paul. "Warne wanted to make sure the big arrangements complimented the vocals. In his words, he wanted to add emotionality and impact to the lyrics."

I ask about the single "We Don't Need Nobody Else," which has generated some controversy in Ireland and England because of an isolated lyric about domestic violence. Early in the song, Fearghal, in a soft voice, says, "I hit you for the first time today. I didn't mean it. It just happened… Christ, we weren't even fighting. I was just annoyed."

"I'm tired of talking about that," says Fearghal.

"Fair enough," I reply. "But, for the record, I don't think the song glorifies violence. It's one of those songs that makes you think about the subject, like Lou Reed's 'Caroline Says,' which you recently covered as a B-Side."

I take a long sip of beer. I'm hoping the Lou Reed comparison will smooth things over. After an uncomfortable moment of silence Paul chimes in and says, "Domestic violence is a big issue that's often covered up in Ireland because of the Catholic Church. Women feel it's their duty to keep the family together. We certainly don't condone abuse. The song's just about that out-of-character, split second of madness."

Paul's words seem to put Fearghal back at ease. Fearghal turns to me and says, "I wasn't trying to be difficult, mate. I'm just tired of all the fuss. I think *Heartworm*'s a very male album. You can tell your readers that. Do you know what I mean? It's very hard for men to express themselves these days. Does that make any sense?"

"It does," I answer.

Paul says, "The song attracted a lot of attention because of the domestic violence theme, but there's more to it than that. A lot of our songs have that dual thing going on. 'We Don't Need Nobody Else' was written at a time when we were really low and found that a lot of our so called friends in the business had deserted us. The chorus was a real defiant statement of intent. We reasoned that if we wrote in an open and honest fashion people would respect it and take it at face value, like those Elvis in Memphis recordings we were talking about at the Rock Garden. We figured that if the writing was as exposed as possible there would be less need for explaining the songs, but in fact the opposite is true."

"Fuck the press," says Myles.

We all laugh.

"So what's the Bono connection?" I ask. "That line about building portholes for Bono so he can gaze out across the bay and sing about mountains cracks me up."

Fearghal chuckles and says, "There's a true story behind that. A mate of mine was working for U2's road crew and we ended up at Bono's house in Killiney. I had to take a piss, so I went to the toilet and there was a porthole right in front of me. It made me wonder if Bono had the house designed like that, so he could gaze out across the bay while taking a piss. It was low to the ground, too, like it was custom built for an extremely short man. I had to hunch down to get a good view."

At this point Colm and Killian return to the dressing room with some of Lou's band. I quickly learn that Lou has a no drugs and alcohol rule for his crew and a few of the guys are desperate to skin up. A joint is passed around and the interview turns into a casual conversation amongst friends. I have enough for my story and I'm starting to buzz from several beers and a few hits of weed. Lou Weed?

Whipping Boy's set is short. Eight songs in just over a half hour, but it's a scorcher. The band are as great as anyone I've ever seen, prime time Bunnymen included. Fearghal, with his curly black hair, looks like the young Tom Hanks in *Bachelor Party*, if Hanks had chosen to wear leather. He appears equally comfortable and confident performing to several thousand Lou Reed fans in a gorgeous theater setting as he did singing to drunk indie kids at Dublin joints like the Rock Garden, Whelan's, and McGonagle's. The new songs like "Twinkle" soar, Paul's guitar effects shooting off like the grand finale of a fireworks show. The older material, including an especially killer rendition of "Valentine 69," sounds defiantly punk rock. I wonder if Lou's crowd remembered their ear plugs. During the set closer, the infamous "We Don't Need Nobody Else," a girl in the audience comes up on stage and drapes a red feather boa over Fearghal's neck, a truly surreal moment.

As the band walks off stage Paul catches my eye and signals for me to follow them backstage. It's a bit *Spinal Tap* but I get past the muscular security guard when Paul and Fearghal (still wearing the boa) tell him I'm with the band. We go to their dressing room where we're greeted by Lou and his band, a few of whom I had met earlier in the day. Introductions are made and I feel like I'm going to faint when I finally shake Lou's hand. I'm star struck but, at the same time, feel like this is an appropriate changing of the guard. In my eyes Whipping Boy should be treated with the same reverence as the Velvet Underground. *Heartworm* is as much of a rebellious response in 1996—a year dominated by post-Nirvana cock rock in the United States and a bland mod revival in Britain—as VU's debut was in 1967 during the summer of love.

The rest of the evening is fantastic, like a slow-motion lucid dream or a perfect trip. More beer is drunk before we go out and stand side stage as the opening chords to "Sweet Jane" kick in. I'm tingling all over. The sound is a little too slick and polished, but damn it, it's still Lou Reed. "Rock and Roll" is next and I tear up when Lou sings, "You know his life was saved by rock 'n' roll." I think about old friends, old girlfriends, and Claire. I'm depressed and alone in Boston, but at this moment, rock 'n' roll is saving me once again. During Lou's set, which goes on for close to three hours, we dash back and forth from the dressing room—more beer, a little weed—to the stage, a few obligatory toilet breaks to relieve our bladders. It's like a mad Benny Hill sketch. I don't know Lou's new material so well, but I seem to be in earshot whenever he plays a classic. "Waiting for the Man," "Satellite of Love," and "Pale Blue Eyes" all hit the spot.

My memory of the rest of the evening is hazy. I'm in a cab and then we're at a party at a hotel suite. Lou's there, so is the famous author Salman Rushdie. I don't recognize Rushdie, but Paul points him out. We joke that we must stay ten feet away from him at all times, just in case we get caught in jihadic crossfire. Fearghal's boa makes the rounds. Even Rushdie is a sport and briefly drapes it over his immaculately tailored suit. The boa is next to me, on my pillow, when I wake up the next afternoon.

Cool Hand Luke Haines

I spend a few hours at the Tate Gallery in the afternoon before heading into Camden. I was hoping to meet up with Dave but he hasn't returned my messages. I remember what Noel Gallagher said and wonder if Dave is passed out in some piss-covered alley or lurid drug den. I'm on the way to the Good Mixer—I figured I'd give the place another shot—when I see a man dressed in a long beige raincoat walking towards me. I can't tell if he's a bum about to solicit me for money, or just a weirdo pervert on his way to a peep show. As our paths cross, I realize he's younger than I initially thought, about my age. He has dirty blonde hair and is wearing a pair of National Health specs. It's Luke Haines from the Auteurs.

The Auteurs' latest *After Murder Park* has been on heavy rotation. I even listened to it on the flight despite two ominous songs about airplanes: "Fear of Flying" and "Light Aircraft on Fire." They're one of the few contemporary bands jiving with me at the moment. Haines hit his stride on this gem. His songs still have that Ray Davies swagger, so prominent on the early Auteurs records, but the mood on the new record is darker. Like Whipping Boy, he's captured something honest, bleak, and raw.

I did a short phone interview with Luke for Spin just before leaving for London. He was cranky and seemed more interested in telling me about his new terrorist-influenced side project called Baader Meinhof than talking about the Auteurs, but I was able to cull a few choice sound bites. Despite Lester Bangs' famous warning that it's perhaps best not to meet your heroes, I turn around and decide to say hello.

Luke says he remembers me. If he doesn't, he's a good liar.

"So what are you doing in London?" he asks.

"I'm here on an assignment. I interviewed Whipping Boy last night. They supported Lou Reed."

"Are they good?"

"They're excellent," I say. "A few of their singles have scraped the Top Forty. You might know 'Twinkle' or 'We Don't Need Nobody Else.'"

"I don't listen to the radio unless I think one of my songs might be on it," says Luke. "It's too full of this Britpop shite that will never die. Look around you, mate."

Luke points his finger at a young couple strutting down Camden High Street.

"They all want to be Damon Fucking Albarn and his twat missus Justine."

I laugh.

"And the northern bands are worse," he says. "Oasis can't write a good song to save their lives. Thick cunts, them and the Verve."

I laugh again before asking, "Can I buy you a drink?"

"I never say no to a drink," says Luke. "As long as we go somewhere where we can avoid these little monkeys."

"You pick the place," I say.

We wander off the High Street into a small restaurant.

"The food here's a bit crap," he says, "but they have good port. Been drinking a lot of that lately."

I tell Luke that I bought the Baader Meinhof single, that I like it.

"The album's just about done," he says. "Nice and short. Just under thirty minutes."

"Do you stick with the terrorist theme throughout?"

"Yes," he says. "Plenty of Baader Meinhof references, plus the PLO, and, even, Carlos the Jackal. There's a track called 'Kill Ramirez.' That was his real name."

"I remember him in the news when I was a kid. All that stuff. PLO, IRA, Red Brigade. My parents used to listen to public radio when I was a kid. They thought it would educate me, but I all I seem to remember from those broadcasts are news about IRA bombings and the Sex Pistols' infamous 1978 tour."

"Not a bad education," chuckles Luke. "Punk rock and terrorism."

I smile and ask Luke what he thinks of Denim, the glam rock group fronted by Lawrence, formerly of Felt. They have a song called "The Osmonds," chock full of seventies references.

"I like it," says Luke, "and I don't like much new music. I hated Felt. 'Primitive Painters' just went on and on, didn't it?"

"I never liked Felt much," I say, "but I do like Denim. Definitely much more than Pulp."

"Pulp's not bad... for being northern. 'Common People' is a decent record. Certainly not as good as say 'Kung Fu

Fighting,' but not bad."

I nearly spit out my port laughing at the reference to the camp seventies hit.

"They're much better than Oasis though," says Luke. "Noel seems to be a decent enough chap, but they're the fucking Rutles, aren't they?"

"I like the first album," I say.

"Your loss," says Luke, "but you like the Auteurs, so you're all right with me."

Luke smiles and takes a long sip of port. We've gone through a few glasses and I'm feeling loopy.

"You know the song 'Tombstone' on *After Murder Park*?" asks Luke.

"Of course," I say. "It's one of my favorites."

"That's my anti-Britpop statement," says Luke.

He sings the opening line: "Taking out the garbage at the Columbia Hotel… we'll take the fucking building out— Baader Meinhof style."

"It's a perfect lead-in to your record," I say.

"Exactly."

I don't tell Luke that I'm actually staying at the Columbia. Part of me wishes that I had a cassette tape rolling now—Luke's quotes are pure dynamite—but then it occurs to me that moments like this shouldn't be frozen and scrutinized.

Luke says he needs to meet a mate who's helping him with

Baader Meinhof mixes so we say our goodbyes. I'm back on Camden High Street and the circus is in full swing. It's nearly midnight. I debate looking for a club—I wonder if Blow Up is still a thing—but the atmosphere is depressing me. I feel old and just want to go back to my room. I have an early flight on Monday. For the first time in my life, I'm not digging the English music scene. These new groups like Ocean Colour Scene and Kula Shaker are karaoke copies of much better sixties bands. How can anyone take this shit seriously?

I cringe at a memory of a Union Jack flag that adorned my bedroom wall when I was nineteen. If someone had asked me what my dream job would have been a decade ago, I would have said rock critic without hesitation, with the same zeal that seventies boys fantasized about becoming Playboy photographers. To some extent my dream did come true. Hell, I interviewed my favorite group yesterday and had drinks with a borderline famous pop star today. Yet, right here, right now, in bustling Camden Town, I feel lost and lonely.

Barfly

When I return from London, I score a temporary job at the publications office at Harvard University. I have bills to pay. It's a chill part-time gig with no expectations. A perfect position for a guy like me without a life plan. I immediately befriend a co-worker named Doug. He's younger than me, just a few years out of college, but we get along well. He digs music (mainly stoner stuff) and likes to party. He invites me to a happy hour at a pub on Mass. Ave. called The People's Republik. Doug says it's not too pretentious by Cambridge standards and they pour a good pint. We're joined by some of his old college buddies from Williams, who have all gravitated to Boston for work.

I'm at the bar getting ready to place my order when I'm greeted by a young woman decked out in full business attire. She has dark hair and skin (probably at least part Hispanic) and a hot body—dangerous curves as an old friend used to say.

"Hi, I'm Sylvia," she says.

"Hi, I'm Drew."

"I usually don't ask guys this, but can I buy you a drink?

"Sure," I say.

"So, what do you do?" she asks.

"I work at Harvard, but I'm a music writer in my spare time. That's my thing."

"Very cool. Who do you write for?"

"Spin and Alternative Press. What about you. What do you do?"

"I'm a lawyer."

The bartender asks what we want. I order a Guinness. She gets a Cape Codder.

"Am I keeping you from anyone?" she asks as she flicks back her hair.

"No. I came here with a friend but he seems pretty occupied now," I say, pointing to a table where Doug and his pals are holding court. "They won't miss me. How about you?"

"I came here with a girlfriend, but she just left. I was going to take a cab home, but decided I wanted to buy you a drink."

"I'm glad you did. I probably would have just gone home and toked up or something."

She laughs. "I can't do that anymore. We have drug testing at my office."

"Ouch."

"Indeed."

We find a small corner table where it's less noisy.

"How long have you been in Boston?" she asks. "You don't have an accent."

"Just a few months."

"Where were you before that?"

"Lots of places, mainly Ireland and England."

I'm not in any kind of mood to talk about myself so I immediately steer things back to her. "How about you? Where are you from?"

"I grew up in Florida. First generation American. My parents are both from Cuba. I came here to go to Wellesley and after that Harvard Law."

"Smart girl."

Smart girl, and very friendly if you catch my drift. She touches my hand a few times during our conversation. I'm not sure if she's aware that she's doing this. I finish my beer and ask if she wants another round.

"Sure," she says.

When I get back to the table, Sylvia's leaning back, her skirt hiked up. I sit down.

"You remind me of a guy I used to know," Sylvia says. "He was tall and thin and had long hair. Only he wore it in a ponytail."

"I hate ponytails," I say, conjuring up an image of Claire and her gray-haired lover Sean.

She asks if I live nearby. I say I do. This seems like déjà vu with Sylvia taking the place of Rachel Blitz. Only the sex isn't as good. She gets off—at least I think she does—but it's taking me forever. Sylvia asks if I'm okay, which irritates me. I'm pissed off and angry that I can't perform and take it out on her. I thrust as hard as I can. Sylvia tells me I'm being too rough. Her desperate tone turns me on. I continue at a reckless pace. I'm on the brink, conjuring up filthy images. Think of someone dirty, I say to myself, focus on some skank. A picture of Rachel Blitz in slut heels, legs spread wide on the Columbia Hotel comforter comes into focus, and I explode into the condom.

The aftermath is depressing. We lie there with nothing to say.

"I should get going," she finally says.

"You can stay if you want," I say, hoping she'll leave.

"I can't. I have to get home. I'm married."

"What the fuck? Why didn't you tell me?"

"You don't seem like the kind of guy who cares."

Sylvia retrieves a wedding band from her purse, slips it on her finger, and leaves the bedroom to phone for a cab. Her words linger in my head long after she leaves. You don't seem like the kind of guy who cares. It depresses me how deep I've sunk since Claire left me. I'm making bad personal choices, drinking far too much, and too depressed to move on.

Maybe that's all that Fearghal was trying to capture in his controversial song; the ugliness of a relationship breaking down. At one point the girl's infidelity is brought into focus and Fearghal spits out in disgust: "It all came out tonight, the queen of drugs broke down and cried, 'cause she'd been shagging her best friend's guy… that's why I'm gazing out of portholes and I'm wondering why."

Bono gazes out of portholes in wonder, Fearghal in despair. Yet, I prefer Fearghal's world of fallen women, drug addicts, drunks, and other would-be contenders to Bono's smug, isolated cocoon occupied by politicians, actors, and supermodels. One U2 record I do like, however, is

Achtung Baby. It's a tad slick, and sonically it's the Edge catching up with bands like My Bloody Valentine and the Stone Roses a few years too late, but Bono's melodies are strong. The man has pipes—that cannot be disputed—but after hearing something as literate as *Heartworm*, it's hard to forgive Bono's clichés on *Achtung Baby*. Wild horses, gypsy hearts, places where the wind calls your name. If this is what a breakup album for the thirty-something set is supposed to sound like, I prefer to stay forever young.

For a time, *Achtung Baby* was the only pop culture link Claire and I had in common. She dove deep into literature when she went back to Trinity, obsessing over Thomas Hardy, her dissertation subject. Relaxation for her—torture for me—was Enya's "Orinoco Flow" on loop, but she loved *Achtung Baby*. We had an inside joke about the track "Until the End of the World." It's a dark song but Claire always used the lyric in a positive light.

"I love you, Claire," I'd say.

"Until the end of the world?" she'd ask back.

Anti-Midas Touch

All men have secrets and here is mine; I got Claire got pregnant six months before her mother died. She had gone off the pill—we were rarely intimate the year before her mother passed away—but one evening, the stars aligned and the old magic was back. We took the DART train to Dalkey to have a drink at the hotel for old time's sake like we did when we were young. We decided to walk to Killiney on the breathtaking coastal road and catch the train home from there. We passed Bono's tower, where he keeps recording equipment, the place with the porthole that Fearghal gazed out of while taking a piss. Bono was outside, smoking a cigarette with Shane McGowan. God knows what the two were up to and if there's any recorded evidence of that evening's collaboration, but it stuck with me that even someone as cool as Shane McGowan has to come to Bono.

"I love you, Drew," she said when we arrived at the station. "Today was beautiful. I wish it could always be like this."

"I love you, too," I said.

"Until the end of the world?"

"Of course."

Claire and I made love that evening, one of the last times we did. A few days later we were back to fighting. Three months later she told me the news. Claire didn't want the child and I didn't have the spine to think things through. I just went with her decision. Abortion is illegal in Ireland, so we went to Manchester, telling friends we were off on a weekend getaway. We opted to fly after a poetic friend, who had once been in a similar predicament, described the ferry ride to England as a cargo of lost souls; a ship full of girls barely old enough to understand the grave decisions they were about to make.

We may never have reached this stage in our relationship if Claire hadn't cheated on me. She and some of her classmates went to a nightclub to celebrate the end of term. She didn't come home until the wee hours of the morning and spent most of the next day on her knees throwing up into the toilet, a first for her. Until then I had been the only one in the house offering regular sacrifices to the porcelain gods.

A few weeks later Claire confessed that she had been untrue. It was early morning and we were still in bed.

"Are you awake?" she asked.

"I am now," I said.

"There's something I need to tell you."

"Okay."

I immediately knew it would be bad. One develops a sixth sense for this kind of thing. Claire told me that after the disco a few of them went to a male classmate's flat. Claire was the last person to leave. She said she was really drunk and that she and her classmate snogged before she gave him a hand job.

"I didn't let him touch me," she said, as if that somehow justified things. It took months before I wanted to sleep with, or even touch, Claire. When I finally did, I got her pregnant. Anti-Midas touch.

I wonder how different my life would be if we had kept the child. I just got a letter from Siobhan with a photo of her new baby boy, Francis. She named him after Frank Black from the Pixies. She says Pat's been an amazing father. He's stopped going out with his mates so much and spends all his time with Francis when he's not playing music. She tells me that Flash have signed to an American label, that there's a real buzz. I'm a little surprised. I always thought they were crap, like a third-rate Radiohead; but then again, the Americans made stars out of Gavin Rossdale and Bush so I suppose anything's possible. I feel sad thinking about Siobhan and what could have been. Perhaps it was for the best. We were true friends, save for that sole moment when we succumbed to loneliness.

Let's Talk About Girls

The evening after my encounter with Sylvia I find myself back at the Red Dragon. Jethro's behind the bar, Loren on a stool, no one else in sight. I sit next to Loren and we bump fists. I order a Tsingtao and when Jethro is out of hearing range I ask Loren if he's the only regular.

"Pretty much," he says with a smile. "Jethro's not too concerned. He makes a lot of money selling other stimulants if you catch my drift."

"That I do. That shit we smoked the last time I was here was lethal. I don't even remember how I got home."

"You and I both, brother."

"You seem a little down," he says.

"More confused," I say. "I got laid last night. Totally out of left field. I feel guilty though. She's a married woman, but she didn't tell me that until we were done. I doubt I'll see her again."

"Fuck her," says Loren, "but you should never feel guilty about pussy. Chicks always know what they want. The biggest mistake I've ever made was putting women on a pedestal. They're stone cold, brother. They're never satisfied. They're always looking for someone who's better; better looking, better car, better income … or they just want to play head games with their partner to make them jealous. The chick you fucked last night was probably looking for a different flavor and you had what she wanted on the menu."

I smirk but feel cold inside. I finish my drink and order a refill. Loren asks about Sylvia.

"She's not my usual type. She's a lawyer. She's hot though. She's curvy with huge tits, kind of borderline chubby. She was pretty dirty, not what you'd expect from a yuppie chick."

"You haven't been around enough of them, brother. Trust me, man. You've been spending too much time with those alternative chicks I bet."

"Guilty as charged," I say. I think about Emily, the Winona Ryder lookalike I met at the Velvet Crush show. I wonder what she's up to.

"See, I have a theory," says Loren. "The more high maintenance and precise a girl's hair style is, the more uptight and high maintenance she is in the bedroom. Those mod girls are the worst. A Mary Quant haircut tells you everything you need to know. Think about it, man. I bet Sylvia has long, wild hair."

"That she does."

Loren laughs and we bump fists. He proceeds to tell me about a threesome he had with two Asian lawyers he met on a business trip.

"They kept taking turns sucking me off," he says. "One of them was doing a better job than her friend, so I'd hold her head down and try to stop her from switching up. The other chick was getting ticked off. Women can be so competitive, even when it comes to sucking off a stranger."

"Man, I thought I was jaded, but you have me beat."

"I have ten years on you, brother, plenty of time to catch up."

Jethro swings by with his pipe. We get high and talk about westerns. I defend Clint Eastwood's spaghetti flicks because, after all, he is Dirty Harry, but Jethro and Loren are firmly in the Sam Peckinpah corner.

I'm sick as a dog the next day, vomiting in a trash can at the Central Square T station, much to the disgust of the other commuters waiting for their trains.

See Emily Play

Nick gives me an assignment to interview Lush. Nick told me that he really dug the Whipping Boy piece, that it was one of the best articles he had read in a long time.

"You have a real knack for championing the underdog," he said. "The story was full of passion and vigor. Even if I had never heard anything by Whipping Boy, I would have rushed out to buy their record."

"Thanks," I said. "I wish I could be a full-time writer. Working for the man can be a drag."

"What are you doing now?"

"I'm an editor at Harvard. Lots of proofreading, easy re-writes, that kind of stuff."

"You should come to New York and work for Spin. We could use some good editors. You'd still be able to write features, too. There aren't any openings now, but there may be some in the fall."

"That would be awesome. My brother comes back at the end of August. It would be perfect timing."

"I'll keep you posted. Let's make this happen."

The Lush gig is at a club called Avalon on Landsdowne, right across the street from the famous Fenway Park, the house that Babe Ruth cursed and vacated for obnoxious chowder-head sports fans. Nick tells me to get there early since the band has other interviews scheduled. There's a small line outside the club when I arrive even though the doors won't open for a good hour. Mainly youthful Anglophiles, those dedicated followers of Face fashion. I walk past a young couple. The guy, who's on the short side, has a haircut like Damon from Blur, while the girl looks like a sexier Justine from Elastica. Her face is far prettier. They remind me of the kids I saw in Camden. Little monkeys, Luke Haines called them. Next to them is Emily. I try to compose myself. She's wearing a Stone Roses T-shirt and colorful beads.

"Hey you," she says in a sultry voice, like she's a femme fatale who stepped out of an old black and white picture.

"Hey," I say, gazing into those eyes. I try to think of something clever to say.

"Oi, the line's back here," says Damon.

"Not if you're interviewing the band," I say, "and please don't say 'Oi' if you're American. That's just plain embarrassing."

The girls giggle and Damon's face turns beet red. Justine steps forward. I can tell she's one of those opportunistic dime a dozen rock 'n' roll chicks, always trolling for boyfriends in bands, backstage passes, and whatever else they can desperately cling to. I had a girlfriend like that once. Funny, how the tables turned. When I was nineteen I was constantly jealous of Christine and the attention she was getting from and giving to older guys. Now I'm in a position to take advantage of a similar scene climber. In Justine's eyes, I might be the guy that could take her one step closer to the British musician of her dreams. I can sense her desperation and motivation, but everything about her, other than her body, repulses me. Maybe it's the short, precise haircut—I remember what Loren told me about alternative girls' haircuts—or maybe I'm finally feeling too old for this shit.

"So who do you write for?" Justine asks as she steps forward.

I look her up and down. Tits spilling out of a tight black Fred Perry, short black skirt, fishnets, and obligatory DM's.

"Mainly Spin," I say.

"That's kind of mainstream," says Damon.

"The paychecks aren't," I say.

Justine laughs and so does Emily. Justine tells me her name, which I immediately forget, and tells me to visit her at the used record store she works at on Newbury Street. I feel sorry for Damon. I can feel his pain. One day he'll chalk it up as a life lesson.

The door man rescues me and says I can go in for the interview. He asks if I have a plus one and, on the spur of the moment, I say, "She's with me," pointing to Emily. Emily looks startled, as if she's possibly wet herself. Justine looks like she's suddenly been crowned Miss America second runner-up when she fully expected to win the pageant. Damon seems to have regained his swagger. Mission accomplished.

Emily and I follow the door guy into the club and he takes us to the dressing room, saying it shouldn't be too long now.

"Feel free to grab a brew," he says, pointing to a cooler full of Rolling Rocks. I take one, twist off the top, and hand it to Emily before grabbing one for myself.

"Thanks," she says. "So, that was a little unexpected."

"It's not like I was going to invite Justine," I say, making my joke public.

Emily laughs. She gets the Elastica reference. "I'd hope not. I know her. She's a piece of work. So, Lush are like one of my favorite bands. This is so cool. I'm Emily by the way."

"I'm Drew. I remember you. We barely got a chance to talk at the Velvet Crush show before some guy dragged you away."

"Oh, God," she says. "That was Ryan. He's my boyfriend."

Emily looks down on the floor, like she's embarrassed to admit this. She's getting to me. I don't care that she's spoken for. I don't see a ring on her finger and I doubt she's hiding one. My emotions are in overdrive. It's sudden and surprising. That smile and those damn eyes. I'm feeling young, dumb, nervous, and possibly in love. Love comes quickly, said those sage British pop poets the Pet Shop Boys.

"So, Drew from Spin magazine, I remember you said you moved here from Ireland. I'm so jealous you got to live there. What were you doing there?"

For a second I feel like I'm talking to Claire again. It's eerie how similar their mannerisms are. Along with the Roses T-shirt (the famous one with the lemon print), she's wearing flared jeans and a pair of low-top black Chuck Taylors—timelessly cool. Claire had the exact same sneakers once. I tell Emily my condensed life story, embellishing all the cool parts, before we're interrupted. It's finally time to talk to Emma and Miki of Lush.

The interview goes well. I'm a little high from the joint I smoked earlier in the afternoon, but all of us seem to be in a mellow mood, so we just chat about random topics ranging from the band's early days when they were compared to My Bloody Valentine to their sudden rise to stardom, at least in the UK, where they grace multiple magazine covers. Emily asks a few questions, too. When it's over she pulls out a disposable camera from her purse and asks if I can take a few snapshots of her posing with Miki and Emma. Emily's glowing.

The show is fantastic. Lush play most of my favorites—"For Love" is especially killer—and I feel happy, in large part because I made someone else happy. I enjoy watching Emily shine.

After the gig, Emily asks where I live.

"Cambridge," I say.

"Me, too," she says. "Feel like getting something to eat?"

"Sure. I'm down."

"Cool," she says. "How does Charlie's Kitchen sound?"

"I've never been there," I say, "but if you like it I'm sure I would too."

"I can't believe you've never been there. You'd so love it. It's like a greasy spoon, but it has an awesome jukebox."

"I'm down," I say for the second time in less than a minute. Christ, I shouldn't be so nervous.

We take the Mass. Ave. bus to Harvard Square and have a nice chat. Emily grew up in Cambridge and is about to graduate from Harvard. She's twenty-one. I know she's probably too young for me, but I rationalize that she must be wise for her years because she goes to an Ivy League school. She says her mom's a shrink and her dad's a jazz musician. She mentions some cats that her old man played with. I know the names even though I know next to nothing about jazz. I ask her what she wants to do with her life.

"I want to be a writer or maybe even a television presenter. I wrote for The Crimson and I'm going to do an internship with the Boston Globe this summer. I'm moving to California in September. Hopefully, I can get a writing job there."

"I'll miss you," I say.

"You don't even know me," she says with a smile.

"I can always tell when important people enter my life," I say. I feel like a tool for taking the mystical route, but I'm a little giddy and trying hard to impress.

"I like you," she says. "You're silly and serious. I can't figure you out."

"Is that good or bad?"

"Good," she says. "I like people who keep me on my toes."

She tousles her hair and I want to place my hands on her cheeks and kiss her.

"So are you moving to California because of Ryan?" I ask.

"Yeah," she says. She looks to the ground as she tells me this. Seems to be a pattern with her whenever she talks about him.

"Ryan's a year older than me," she says. "He graduated from Harvard last year. He just finished his first year at Stanford Law. He's doing an internship in San Francisco now. I'm moving in with him in September. He was home for Christmas break when you met him. He's not that into music. He can get pretty cranky at concerts."

"I won't bring him up again," I say. "I didn't mean to be nosy. I hope he knows how lucky he is."

She laughs and says, you don't even know me for the second time.

"So how did you get into writing?" she asks.

I tell her about my old friend PJ. He was the catalyst. PJ and I grew up together in Ann Arbor. The two of us drifted apart the year before I went to England when he got into hard drugs. I still wonder if there was anything I could have done to steer him off that destructive course. Too many dead friends, too many dead ends. I tell Emily how PJ lied to get us back stage at a Sisters of Mercy show, claiming I was a journalist.

"That was in Detroit back in 1984 and PJ told their manager I wrote for Spin. The dude got us backstage and I interviewed the band. I ended up getting the piece published for my college newspaper, in part because PJ was the editor's pot dealer. It's really cool that you're a writer, too. I feel like I've come full circle. I've been looking for a way to pay PJ back, now that I really do write for Spin."

"That's really sweet," she says. "I owe you one."

Emily was right. Charlie's is a cool dive that doesn't fit in with the rest of the Harvard Square aesthetic. Emily tells me to order the grilled cheese. I get that, plus a beer and a shot. I need to get my buzz back. She orders a beer but passes on the shot.

"I like you Drew, but I can tell that you're hurting. You can tell me what's wrong if you want to. You can trust me. Sorry if I sound like a psychologist. Blame it on having a mom who's a shrink."

"Is it that obvious? Are you psychotic?"

Emily looks puzzled.

"Oh, Christ, I mean psychic." I smile, as I quickly correct myself.

She laughs and takes my hand and looks straight into my eyes.

"I've been accused of being psychic before, but never psychotic! Seriously though you can talk to me."

I tell Emily everything. It feels like therapy.

"That's so sad," she says. "It must feel terrible to get left by someone you love."

"It is," I say. "I keep blaming myself for not seeing the signs. Claire snapped when her mom died. She stopped going to classes and started hanging out at a new age center, which, in retrospect, seems more like a cult. They were into things like past life regression and healing with crystals. Claire was convinced that she could communicate with her mom from beyond the grave."

"Wow, that's pretty far out," says Emily.

"Yeah, I tried to support her even though I knew it was completely wacky. Right before she left she gave a bunch of her stuff away to friends. I should have seen the signs. She kept talking about downsizing her life and getting more in touch with her spiritual being."

I tell Emily how Claire and I would take trips to sacred sites like the ancient burial mound at Newgrange. Claire told me she could see portals to other dimensions and could step through any time she wanted. Her words sounded like threats. We would see her dad most weekends in Belfast. As the months passed after Ann's death, he started to get back to his old self, but Claire remained lost. Her dad took me aside at one point and begged me to take care of her. "Of course," I said. "She's the love of my life."

Claire wouldn't shut up about the center and Sean in particular. She claimed that the two of them had a past-life bond and were meant to be together again. I tell Emily that despite all this, I still feel guilty.

"I keep thinking I should have done more. God knows I tried. She wouldn't listen to me or any of her old friends. She kept saying how her new friends were the only people who understood her."

I'm shaking and ask the waitress for another shot and the check.

"Look, Emily, I'm sorry for laying this on you. You're the first person I've felt comfortable enough to open up to since I've moved here."

"It's okay," she says. What else can she say?

We go outside and Emily takes my hand. I'm shaking and hold back tears.

"Jesus, I'm a mess," I say.

"It's okay," she says. "Come home with me, I'm just around the corner. I don't want to leave you alone. I have a couch you can sleep on."

Emily lives in a studio apartment near the Harvard campus. I feel like I'm twenty-one again and imagine I'm back at Essex. Emily's apartment reminds me of Claire's old room, updated for a new decade with posters of the Stone Roses, Blur, Primal Scream, and Radiohead in lieu of the

Jesus and Mary Chain, Sisters of Mercy, and Psychedelic Furs. I feel nostalgic and creepy. I think of that line about girls from *Dazed and Confused*: I get older, they stay the same age.

I curl up on the tiny couch while Emily goes to the bathroom to wash up. She comes out wearing nothing but her baggy Stone Roses T-shirt, which fits her like a mini dress. She walks over to me.

"On second thought, that couch is pretty crappy," she says. "You can sleep with me."

I hesitate for a second, wondering if I missed some obvious signal. She laughs. "Don't worry, I won't bite."

It's purely platonic. I lie on my back while she curls up next to me, her head nestled near my chest, arms holding me tightly. "It's going to be okay, Drew," she says.

I wish her words were true, but I can't sleep, even though I'm polluted on cheap beer and bourbon. All I can think about is Claire at the funeral. I held her hand all day, guiding her like a small child, constantly telling her I loved her. I was in a daze too, overwhelmed by an endless procession of crying women and stern men in black suits, buzzing from multiple cups of coffee spiked with Bushmills.

Emily wakes me up in the morning with a cup of Joe that she's brought over from a nearby Dunkin' Donuts.

"I assume you like coffee," she says. Emily looks hot even when she hasn't made herself up. She's wearing a black skirt and a Lush T-shirt that she bought at the show last night.

"I live for caffeine," I say. "Christ, I didn't even hear you get up. What time is it?"

"It's only 7:30. I tend to wake up early even when I go to bed late."

"Speed freak, eh?" I laugh.

She laughs too. "No, just coffee for me, but you should see some of my classmates."

"I believe it. I knew a few stress cases in my time. I'm not a morning person at all."

"I can tell," she says. "You were out cold. You kept talking in your sleep, like you were having a violent dream."

"I don't remember a thing. Hope I wasn't keeping you up too much."

"No, that's okay. I'm just glad you're okay now. You were kind of a wreck last night."

"Sorry about that."

"It's okay. It's all good. Glad I could be of some help."

"Thanks again for that. I owe you one."

"I'll take you up some time."

She smiles, before continuing. "I need to get ready for work. You can stay and walk me to the T if you want to."

"I'd like that."

I get dressed while Emily changes in the bathroom. She comes out looking grown-up, well, maybe more like a kid playing grown-up, in a skirt, nicely pressed white blouse, and a pair of Doc Marten Mary Jane's. She has a meeting with her new boss at The Globe before classes today, she says.

"You look nice," I say. "Like a junior reporter or something."

She playfully smacks me on the shoulder and says, "This girl's got to make a living. I'm not lucky enough to write for music magazines and sleep whenever I want to."

I'm not sure if that was meant to be a dig, so I let it slide.

"We better get going," she says.

"Cool. I'm good."

We exchange phone numbers and she asks if I want to see a show at the Middle East on Saturday night. "They're a local band called the Curtain Society. Have you heard of them?"

"No," I say.

"I think you'd like them. They remind me of the Cure."

"Cool."

"Then it's a date."

Emily smiles. As we walk to the Harvard Square T station, she chats endlessly about UK buzz bands like Cast, Heavy Stereo, and Mansun. She even mentions Concealer. I don't tell her about Rachel Blitz. Emily seems to take every word written in the NME and Melody Maker to be the gospel truth, like I used to.

She hugs me at the station and then, rather impulsively, gives me a quick peck on the lips.

"We have so much to talk about," she says.

I watch her glide down the escalator until she disappears from sight.

Reefer Madness

That evening I go to the Red Dragon for the first time in a few weeks.

"Long time," says Loren.

"Yeah, I know. I keep meaning to pop by, but I've been busy writing."

"No need to apologize for bailing on this place. Jethro and I forgive you."

He laughs. "So what have you been working on?" he asks.

I tell him about the Lush interview and my adventures with Whipping Boy in London. He seems more excited about my writing than I am. Don't get me wrong. I'm proud that I've stuck to my guns and grinded out a life as a journalist, but lately I've been shit scared about the future. I'm thirty-one and I don't have a career, retirement plan, health insurance, or a woman. If something doesn't pan out with Spin in the fall, perhaps I'll have to walk away from it all and reinvent myself. The empty bar doesn't help my mood. On the song "Personality," Fearghal sings, "People grow old. They get bored. They forget to take a risk." But, that's never been my problem. I've been taking bullets for rock 'n' roll since my teens.

"So, does anyone ever come here?" I ask.

Loren and Jethro laugh before Loren says, "Dude, there was a chick in here just a little while ago. Pretty cute from what I could tell. I didn't get that good of a look. She just walked in and out like she was trying to find someone."

"Damn," I say. "I feel sorry for anyone looking for someone here. No offense to you guys."

"None taken," says Loren. "I'm here because I want to forget about life, not live it. What else has been going on with you?"

I tell him about Emily and let it slip that I really like her. "Hell, I probably shouldn't waste my time on her. She's got a boyfriend. You'd probably tell me to just keep on banging the lawyer, right? Hang on to a sure thing."

"Probably the safer bet, but I've got some life left in my heart, brother. I'm kind of a romantic misogynist if you catch my drift. I like the chase and, at times, I really do like women, but, man, they always end up disappointing me. You need to be careful of the young ones. One minute they'll be way into you and the next day you're yesterday's papers."

"I like the chase, too," I say, "but I live for those moments when I can just be happy with someone and freeze time. It always goes by too fast though, like a good drug buzz or something."

"Speaking of, let's get another round."

Loren signals to Jethro to bring over some Tsingtaos and shots and then walks over to the jukebox and selects some tunes from a Leonard Cohen best-of: "Suzanne," "Chelsea Hotel," and "So Long, Marianne." Good music to bum out to, he says. I wonder if Emily likes Leonard Cohen. She seems too happy and focused to get depressed. It's like she already has her life figured out.

I try to reiterate these thoughts to Loren and he listens

semi-attentively, before saying, "The thing is with young chicks, especially the really smart ones like your lady, is they know what they want and they're pretty ruthless about getting it. They might like you and even sleep with you, but they'll drop you like a bad habit with no regrets. I'm sure Emily's into you. You're a good-looking, mysterious dude and all that, but it's biology, brother. No matter how successful they are, they want a dude who's more successful, or they're just bat shit crazy."

He proceeds to tell me a story about a young girl he dated a few years ago. "She was this hot chick straight out of college who was working at my bank. We hooked up a few times, and the sex was really good, so I was riding it out. One night I was at her apartment and we were doing bong hits and making out and then she asked me to go down on her. I think I took too big of a hit or something because as soon as I got in between her legs I felt nauseous and had to run to the bathroom to throw up. Oh man was she pissed. She screamed at me to get out and started throwing stuff at me while I was getting dressed."

We all laugh but Loren's earlier line about biology feels like a blow. Christ, I need another drink, something to numb me. I try to think about something else. I wonder what Emily's doing right know, probably fast asleep in that little studio apartment of hers, no doubt in a hurry to move on to something bigger and better, not realizing how great she has it right now. Or maybe I'm just some pathetic Peter Pan type, locked in at twenty-one for life. I fucked up with Claire. Maybe I'd get it right this time with Emily if I ever get a chance. A girl like her might force me to grow up. Rock 'n' roll saved my life once, made me a rebel, but right now I feel like it's backfired on me. I'm a wreck.

I finish my beer and Loren and Jethro want to get stoned. I take a few hits and get gone. Real, real gone.

Red Guitars and Broken Hearts

On Saturday afternoon I meet Emily at Dunkin' Donuts. We grab some coffees and make our way through Harvard Square, checking out several used record stores and the three chains: Tower, HMV, and the locally owned Newbury Comics, which is by far the best of the bunch. I buy a new Brian Jonestown Massacre record, but nothing else. I have stacks of promos that I haven't listened to piling up at the apartment. I don't need more clutter. Emily buys a selection of import singles by Pulp, Cast, Charlatans, Oasis, Blur, and Concealer. She tells me that Electrafixion, a newish band fronted by Ian and Will from Echo and the Bunnymen (for all intents and purposes, Bunnymen mark two) will be in Boston in June and maybe I want to join her? I say sure, liking the idea that she wants me in her life for at least a few more weeks.

Emily wants to eat at Charlie's again, so we stop there before heading to the Middle East. I compliment her for wearing an old New Order tour T-shirt, mentioning that I saw them a few times in the eighties. Emily's T-shirt is bright pink and features a star logo next to the number 89, the words New Order USA printed below.

"Wow, you're lucky," she says. "I keep forgetting that you're old."

I cringe.

"Sorry," she says. "I didn't mean it in a bad way. You don't look old at all. You look really good. I mean it. I like older guys." The sultry femme fatale voice kicks in again.

"Glad to have your stamp of approval."

She reaches into her purse and says, "I have something for you." She hands me a cassette. "It's just a mix tape. You probably know all the bands, but I think it flows really well."

"Thanks," I say. "I probably don't know half of it to be honest. I don't read magazines as much as I used to. I'm not as cool as you think I am."

"Yeah, you got to interview Lush. Such a loser," she says as she punches my shoulder playfully.

"Well, you're pretty cool yourself," I say. "Where did you get the T-shirt?"

"Ryan found it for me in San Francisco at some thrift shop. I just got it in the mail yesterday."

"It's really nice," I say, trying not to sound deflated. I keep forgetting that she's in a long distance relationship. I even considered making Emily a tape but right now I'm glad I didn't. That would have been sad, desperate, and clingy. Still, I can't help but wonder what I might have included. I immediately think of the Ultra Vivid Scene tune "Special One" with Kurt Ralske's killer melody and Kim Deal's ace backing vocals, a dead-on perfect song. I wish Emily was my special one. See? Sad, desperate, and clingy.

Nevertheless I do tell her how great she looks for about the third time.

"That's sweet of you to say, but don't like me too much. It'll make it harder for me to leave," she says. It's driving me nuts how she alternates between flirting and shutting me down.

"Do you really have to?" I ask.

"I need to leave Cambridge. I've been here too long. My family situation isn't the best."

"Anything you want to talk about?"

"Yeah. I promise I will some time." She pauses to collect her thoughts. "I really like you Drew. I wish we met under different circumstances. Let's just try to be friends and not get all heavy on each other."

"I can do that. So how about those Red Sox?"

She laughs and we're back to being okay, at least that's what I tell myself. I think about Siobhan and our missed timing and wonder if I'm headed for a repeat.

The Curtain Society are as good as Emily promised, a dynamic trio that reminds me of legendary British bands like the Cure, Chameleons, and My Bloody Valentine. After the show she asks if I want to walk back to Harvard Square instead of taking the bus. I say sure. She opens up and tells me about her mom and dad.

"I feel like they're only married because they think they're supposed to be for my sake. My parents are like total opposites. My mom was the big academic achiever. She moved here from a small town to go to Radcliffe and met my dad right after she graduated. He's like ten years older. She met him at some concert his band was playing at and they hooked up. She got pregnant with me and they got married. I don't think anyone on my mom's side of the family expected it to last, but he's stuck around."

"That doesn't sound so bad."

"Well, it wasn't until my mom went back to school and

got her graduate degree. Now she's a really successful psychologist and I think it appalls her that my dad just wants to play music. He doesn't go on tour like he used to, so it's not a money-making thing anymore, but I mean that's all that he loves to do. I don't know why my mom can't let it go. They're not hurting for money. She was always on my case as a kid because she thought I spent too much time listening to music and that my dad was a bad influence. I was pretty much forced to become a straight-A student out of fear of getting my cassettes and CDs taken away."

"My dad and brother are professors, and my mom is an editor, so I can definitely relate."

"So how did you get into music?" she asks.

"It kind of just happened by accident. I used to be a really good runner, like good enough to run for my college team, but I just burned out on that. I quit the team and started hanging out with outcasts. I started writing for my college paper and then studied abroad, and that sealed the deal for me."

"I wish I could have done that. I thought about applying to grad school at Oxford or Cambridge."

"You should do that. You'd love it there."

"Maybe someday. California should be fun."

We're getting close to her place and I don't want the evening to end so I ask her if she wants to get more coffee. She does, so we go to this trendy place in Harvard Square, which also doubles as a hookah bar. The place is an interesting mix of college kids, professors drinking coffee and tea, and Middle Eastern men sucking on long pipes.

"So do you want to be a music journalist?" I ask.

"That's what I usually write about, but I'd like to be more versatile and cover movies and television too. I love old movies."

"Like what?" I ask.

"A lot of the old black and white romantic comedies. My parents would always take me to the Brattle Theatre. Have you ever been there?"

"No."

"We should go some time. It's right down the block from here."

"Cool. So what other music do you like besides all the Britpop bands?"

"My first favorite band was R.E.M. *Document* came out when I was in ninth grade. I remember buying 'The One I Love' on a cassette single. I don't like them so much anymore. They're too normal now. What about you? Any hot tips for me?"

"I'm kind of jaded on new bands other than Whipping Boy and the Auteurs. I've always loved Primal Scream though. Their last record is great."

"It's too hard rock for me. I like *Screamadelica* more."

"I do too, but I dig their rock 'n' roll side. 'Rocks' is a classic. It reminds me of the Stones. I keep forgetting I'm an old man."

She laughs. "So who's your all-time favorite band if you had to pick one?"

"The Jesus and Mary Chain though I don't like *Stoned & Dethroned* so much. *Honey's Dead* is perfect though, nearly as good as *Psychocandy* in my book. That band made me not want to grow up."

A waitress comes by to pick up our dishes and says they're closing up, so we head out. I walk Emily back to her place, hoping she might invite me in, but kind of knowing she won't. I remember what she said earlier about not wanting to get heavy. When we get to her door I give her a hug. She kisses me, letting it linger for a couple of seconds before pulling back.

"I'm sorry," she says.

"For what?"

"I don't want to give you mixed signals, but I really like you. I keep giving you signals. I'm so sorry."

"It's okay. I like you, too." I put my hand on her shoulder to reassure her before I leave.

Christ, I'm in the fucking friend zone. As I walk home I wonder what Loren is up to. I realize I don't have his number. I decide I don't want to get wasted, so I take a long roundabout way home, wishing I had music to keep me company. Something sad, like the red guitars and broken hearts Fearghal sings about.

Long walks with my Walkman were my sanctuary that last year in Dublin. Catherine Wheel's *Chrome* was a popular choice on strolls through Ballsbridge and Dublin city center. I was sleeping on the living room couch by then; "Love Will Tear Us Apart" kind of stuff. When I first got into Joy Division as a teen I was still a virgin, so I never quite understood the song's depth. I do now. Anyone who has been in a marriage or long-term relationship winces when they hear Ian Curtis' words: "Why is the bedroom so cold? You've turned away on your side." "Pain" was the

"Love Will Tear Us Apart" for me on Chrome. My eyes would water every time the opening verse kicked in. "Before the summer fell I already knew. She said I was more than dead, but I already knew."

When I get home I pour myself a glass of water and put on the Rolling Stones' *Hot Rocks*, the first record I bought as a kid with my own money. I lie back in bed and my mind races back to another time and another place. When I was young, my favorite sport was basketball, but I was never good enough to make the junior high team. Another kid told me about a drill he learned at a summer basketball camp. You lie back in bed, holding a basketball in a shooting position, and flick it up in the air, catch, and repeat for about twenty minutes. I would do this drill every night as I listened to an album on my stereo, usually one of the sides from *Hot Rocks*. I'd stare at the giant Pete Maravich poster on my wall, gazing at his long hair and floppy socks, wishing that I, too, could be an NBA all-star. Despite the extra practice, I got cut from the team again in the eighth grade and, soon after that, took up track and field, a sport I excelled at. Even so, for the next few years I'd still perform that basketball drill most evenings, even after becoming an all-state runner. It was a stress release button. Rolling Stones and Pistol Pete. There's no basketball at the Cambridge condo and my old Pistol Pete poster is long gone, but the Rolling Stones suffice.

Echoes of the Bunnymen

The next few weeks are uneventful. I fall into a routine of writing, working at Harvard, and hanging out with Emily as much as she'll let me. I hate it that I'm doing most of the chasing. I feel like a clingy, insecure teenager. I desperately want to impress her, but I'm starting to realize that a thirty-one-year-old music journalist isn't anything to write home about, especially to a Harvard chick. For a few scary days I contemplate going to graduate school before concluding that would be as bizarre as joining the French Foreign Legion.

Sometimes when I hang out with Emily I feel like I'm her gay best friend. No matter what anyone might tell you, it's nearly impossible to be friends with a woman. Siobhan and I were stone pals and we still had our slip ups. With opposite sex friendships it's inevitable that one of you will have an unrequited romantic interest. I know Emily finds me attractive. More often than not she'll kiss me good-bye on the lips, showing feelings stronger than friendship. Still, it's hard to gauge if things could work out. The age gap doesn't bother me so much because I know most girls my age don't have a lot of time for 'old' rock 'n' rollers like me. I wince remembering the first time Claire called me that. I'll start to worry if I'm still chasing twenty-year-olds when I'm forty.

Emily and I see Electrafixion at Axis in June. I ask Nick if I can do an interview with Ian and Will, but he tells me that Sire just dropped the band so it isn't in Spin's interest to run the story. They can only feature bands on labels who actually advertise in the magazine, he explains. In other words, it's the old features-for-ad-space swindle.

Nick senses my disappointment and says, "Music can be an ugly business, but it still beats working a real job. You'll see what I mean when you come to New York. Besides, I hear the Bunnymen are going to reform."

True to Nick's prophecy, Electrafixion cover a good number of the old classics. They play "Rescue," "Villiers Terrace," "Killing Moon," and an absolutely shit hot extended version of "Do It Clean." Ian hasn't lost any of his old moves; obligatory cigarette dangling from his mouth as the band morphs into James Brown's "Sex Machine," followed by Gerry and the Pacemaker's "Ferry Across The Mersey," before bringing it all back home again. Do it fucking clean. They even cover songs by the two best bands of the sixties: the Stooges "Loose" and Velvet Underground "Pale Blue Eyes." The latter takes me to the Whipping Boy show in London, reawaking Lou's powerful rendition.

Emily and I get coffee in Harvard Square before calling it a night. She's in good spirits, telling me about her latest favorite band Cast, whose singer, John Powers, used to be in the La's. I tell her how much I love the La's and we end up having a discussion about Lee Mavers, speculating if he'll ever make another record. The discussion then moves to Whipping Boy when Emily tells me that she bought *Heartworm* on my recommendation and that she really likes it. I realize that I have a letter from Paul in my pocket and I read her an excerpt:

> *Remember Lou's bass player Fernando? One day we were watching Lou's band soundcheck and Myles shouted at him, 'Can you hear the drums, Fernando?' He didn't get the Abba reference but it cracked us up. We also did a French live TV show with Lou*

and Elvis Costello. I don't think I have ever been more nervous performing live—the relief when it was over was overwhelming. Afterwards, Fearghal was interviewed with Lou and Elvis, and Lou said some lovely things about us. The very last show of the tour in Birmingham we dared Fearghal and our tour manager to dress up as women for the whole day. Colm decided he would join in, so for the day, they all dressed as very unattractive women. We passed Lou in the venue and he saw the guys and I wondered, did he think this drag act was in any way us taking the piss? We performed onstage like that too—me and Myles wrapped cling film around our heads, so we looked like a right troupe of weirdoes!

Emily reminds me so much of Claire at that age with her overzealous enthusiasm for music and life. The first time I talked to Claire was at a Jesus and Mary Chain concert at the end of 1985. I wonder what might happen if things work out with Emily. Would she end up seeing me as an old rock 'n' roller, too?

I'm pondering this when Emily says, "Oh my God, my parents just walked in. What are they doing out so late? This is so embarrassing."

"Should we duck under the table?"

I'm only half kidding. They walk over to our table. Emily makes the introductions and asks if they want to join us. Her parents are what I expect. Dad is tall and thin with long gray hair, wearing jeans and a nice black blazer. Dapper like a jazz cat should be. He's polite and soft-spoken, a super mellow guy. I instantly like him. Mom doesn't seem crazy about me. She barely acknowledges my presence, immediately zeroing in on her daughter.

"Why are you up so late?" she asks.

"I was at a concert. Why are you out so late?" Emily teases back.

"We saw a movie at the Brattle Theatre. A bit past my bed time, but you know your father and *The Maltese Falcon*."

"That's a great flick," I say. "I love Hammett. Have you read the novels?"

"Fuck yeah," says dad.

Emily and I laugh. Mom frowns and throws dad a dagger.

"So what do you do for a living Drew? How do you know Emily?" asks mom.

"I'm a writer. Mainly Spin. Emily and I met at a concert…"

"He interviewed Lush. I got to meet them. It was so cool," says Emily.

"That's nice," says dad. "Emily could use friends with real world writing experience. Did you go to a fancy place like Harvard, Drew?"

I pick up on dad's sarcasm. So does mom.

"What do you care?" mom asks. "It's not like you're paying for Emily's education."

Ouch. This is getting a little too Liz Taylor and Richard Burton for me.

"I went to Michigan," I say. "I also studied in England."

Dad lights up and proceeds to tell me stories about London clubs he played at, how he once jammed with Charlie Watts. Mom abruptly changes the subject.

"So how's Ryan? Is he still visiting in July?"

Emily looks uncomfortable. I had no idea Ryan was visiting. Obviously she didn't want me to know.

"He's fine," she says after taking a long pause. "He's still coming."

"I can't wait to see him again," says mom. "He's such a nice boy."

"I'm so sorry about that," Emily says after her parents leave. "My mom can be a real bitch."

"It's okay. I can tell she doesn't like me. Your dad's cool though."

"Everyone likes him. I can tell he really likes you, too, Drew. I don't know what got into my mom. She's usually not that bad. I don't think she appreciated seeing me with another guy. She's infatuated with Ryan."

Fade Into You

Emily phones later in the week. She's drunk. She's been at a happy hour in a Boston bar with co-workers and asks if I want to meet her somewhere. I say sure. We agree to meet at a pub near the MIT campus called Miracle of Science, a good halfway point.

She's there when I arrive, frantically waving her arms at me.

"I'm glad you could make it, Drew. I didn't think you would come."

"Of course I would. Why wouldn't I?"

"I thought my mom might have scared you off or something. She doesn't like you," she says with a slight slur.

"Yeah, I could tell. Did she actually say something?"

"Yeah. She called me this morning. She thinks you're a bad influence."

"Do you?"

"Of course not, silly."

Sometimes the easiest way into a girl's heart is to be the kind of guy mom doesn't like. I've had countless friends complain to me about girls' mothers, especially ones who talk to their daughters on a daily basis. Emily's mom seems to be that type. She's probably already planned the wedding to Ryan.

I order a beer. Emily tells me to get a shot, too, saying I need to catch up. I tell her to order some food because she's pretty ripped. She orders a beer instead.

"You've never invited me to your apartment, Drew. I thought you liked me?"

"Of course I like you," I say. "We've just always ended up near your place."

"Can we go to your place now? I want to see your records."

"Are you coming on to me?" I tease. "Is that like when a guy asks a girl if she wants to see his etchings?"

She laughs. "Well, do you have any?"

We cab it to my apartment. She practically attacks me when we get inside. We make out for a few minutes in the hallway. My mind is racing, wondering what got into her. Did something happen with Ryan or does she just want a rebellious one-night stand to get back at her mom? This is everything I wanted but it's not happening according to plan. My strategy has been to gradually win over Emily until she realizes she has more in common with me than Ryan.

When we get into my living room, she rifles through my records and CDs. She selects the Jesus and Mary Chain *Honey's Dead* and quickly undresses in front of me, dancing to the sexy beats of "Reverence." She signals for me to follow her into the bedroom. "Teenage Lust" is on now. She continues her striptease. The situation is hot, but feels borderline inappropriate. Maybe it's the song, I think, as I listen to Jim Reid's words: "Little skinny girl, she's doing it for the first time. Little skinny girl, she's doing it and it feels fine." I sit down on the bad, enjoying Emily's gyrations, almost too shocked to react. She stops mid-song.

"Don't you think I'm sexy, Drew?"

"Of course I do. I'm enjoying the show."

She's not convinced.

"Everyone just thinks I'm cute. Ryan thinks I'm cute... the cute rebellious girl with the eyebrow piercing who likes all the silly bands. Is that how you see me?"

I jolt off the bed and kiss her.

When we stop to catch our breath she says, "Wow. No one has ever kissed me like that. I didn't realize you had so much passion."

"I have tons of it. I've been crazy about you from the moment I met you."

She tugs on my shirt and says, "Prove it."

She does look really cute at this moment, but I don't dare tell her so. Instead, I attack her like I'm an inmate on his monthly conjugal. Afterward we're lying in bed, both of us too nervous to speak. I lean over and kiss her softly. I want to tell her that I love her but I know it's too early and that I'd probably freak her out, so I bite my tongue.

"I hope you won't judge me, Drew," she says.

"What do you mean?"

"Like I hope you don't think I'm a slut or something. I've never cheated on Ryan or anything, but I really like you and I'm sick of everyone expecting me to be little miss perfect, like my mom. And besides things aren't that great with Ryan. He was like my first real boyfriend, but we don't have that much in common now."

"You don't have to prove anything to me. I like you the way you are."

I feel less guilty about sleeping with Emily now that I know where things stand with her and Ryan, but I'm not terribly proud of myself and the gray area choices I've made lately. First Sylvia and now this. My moral compass has gone haywire since Claire left.

"Thanks," she says as she leans over to kiss me. "You're almost too mellow, Drew, like you lock away everything inside."

"I just want to be happy and I hope I can make you happy."

"I wish it could be that easy for us. I've got two years invested in Ryan, even if we're in a rut. It's hard to just stop. And you're not even divorced yet, are you?"

"No," I say. "I don't even know where Claire is."

"Do you still talk to her dad? Does he know where she is?"

"I imagine so. The last time I talked to him was just after Christmas. He was really worried about her."

"When was the last time you talked to her?"

"Do you really want to talk about this?"

"We have to sometime if we're going to have a future."

"Last year was the last time I talked to her. I tried calling her this spring, but no one seems to know where she lives now."

"That's too bad," Emily says.

I don't know how to respond, so Emily continues. "I mean

it's too bad because I know you were happy once. I know I'm really young but I do know what it feels like to be happy and I know what it feels when everything is wrong. The first year with Ryan was really good and then he suddenly got it into his head that he had to go to law school. I said that I'd support him but now I'm not so sure I want that kind of life."

"How do you feel now? I mean outside of all the heavy shit we've been talking about. Like with us. I won't go all goofy and stalk you. I promise."

She laughs and says, "I feel happy. Is that enough?"

The next morning Emily wakes me up and asks, "Have you ever done mushrooms?"

This girl is full of surprises.

"A few times," I say. "Why? Do you have some?"

"A friend does. Well, her boyfriend does. He's a real stoner. She's house-sitting for her parents next weekend and they invited me over, but she just found out she has to take a drug test for a job."

"It's good she found out now."

"Yeah. She said I could have the mushrooms if I wanted them. Do you want to take a trip?" She giggles. "I've never done anything really bad. It can be like our first real date."

"Wow, you've turned into quite the bad girl," I tease.

"I know, right. Sleeping with a married man and now drugs. Heavens to Betsy, what would mother think?"

"So we have a relationship now?"

"Unless you have regrets. I have to figure out how to break it to Ryan. He's visiting next month. That's going to be awkward. I don't want to think about it," she says with a groan.

"Sorry."

"Well, you're not off the hook either. You need to track down that wife of yours. It's kind of hot sleeping with a married man and all, but that's going to get old real fast."

"Noted."

We make love again. Afterward she asks if I like Mazzy Star.

"I know you'll think it's silly," she says, "but I really want to hear 'Fade Into You' while I lie next to you. I have the CD in my purse."

She pops in the CD and snuggles next to me, kissing me on the lips as Hope Sandoval belts out the chorus, "Fade into you, strange you never knew."

"I love you," I say. The words just come out.

"I love you, too, Drew. You treat me right."

"What do you mean?"

"Like you're sweet when we hang out, but a stronger side comes out when we're intimate, like you really want me. It's nice."

"It's because I do."

"Ryan doesn't seem to want me anymore. I visited him during spring break and he barely touched me... Sorry for bringing him up again. I don't want to spoil this moment."

She gets up, puts "Fade Into You" on the player again, and gets back under the covers. This time she holds me tight, like a scared child.

Mushrooms and Methodrone

Emily arrives early on Saturday evening. She's wearing a floral sixties-style sleeveless dress and a stylish hat that looks like something Marianne Faithfull or the Shrimpton sisters might have worn.

"You look fantastic," I say, before kissing her.

"Thanks. I feel a bit too much like a hippie, but I wanted to get into character. I feel like I'm in a school play or something."

"Just wait till the mushrooms kick in."

"So when do we start?"

"Any time," I say. "Don't operate any heavy machinery."

She giggles. We're about halfway through *Screamadelica* when the pizza topped with special mushrooms works its magic. I'm playing the import CD with the extended bass-heavy, psychedelic version of "Come Together," the one with the Jessie Jackson samples. I feel high and tell Emily.

She laughs. "The mushrooms are from a farm in Vermont."

"Ben and Jerry's?" I ask.

She laughs again and soon we're both in hysterics. We start to make out, but we're too high to get beyond the sloppy kissing stage. She gets up and says she wants to see the balcony.

I don't know how long we gaze at the stars. It could have

been twenty minutes and it could have been two hours. Our hands are locked the whole time and I don't want to move. Emily breaks the mystical silence by loudly announcing that she has to pee.

We go inside. When Emily is finished, she combs through my record collection.

"Play me something cool," she says. "Play me something I haven't heard before." She's acting like a sugared-up kid in a toy store.

"Have you heard this?" I ask. I hand her a CD by the Brian Jonestown Massacre. It's called *Methodrone*.

"No," she says. "Are they English? The cover art looks like a Slowdive record."

"They're from San Francisco," I say, "but this is way better than all that Britpop shit the man is spoon-feeding us."

Methodrone is majestic. The first half is full of fuzzy psychedelic rockers and Emily and I are dancing barefoot— just like the Patti Smith song—gazing into each other's eyes. I'm fully convinced I'm in love with her, that she's the one. When the vibe on the record gets more introspective we move to the couch and kiss some more, stopping from time to time just to laugh and smile.

"Do you have any weed?" she asks as she runs her fingers through my hair. "You look like the kind of guy who always has weed." I smile inside. The kind of guy who always has weed has a nicer ring than the kind of guy who doesn't care.

"I do," I say. "It's strong."

I pack a bowl and we take a few hits. Emily takes off her

dress. She's not wearing a bra. We start to kiss again for the umpteenth time, but she's fading fast. She passes out and I'm left holding her, sound asleep, in my arms. I smile to myself, remembering that scene in *Animal House*. Eventually I get up and walk to the kitchen. I'm in dire need of water. The phone rings. The connection is bad like it's a transatlantic call or something. It's Loren. I don't remember giving him my number, but, obviously, I must have. He's at the Red Dragon and asks if I wants to stop by.

"I can't, man. I have company."

"Emily?"

"Yeah."

"This chick was here a while ago. She was looking for you brother."

"Come on, man. Don't fuck with me. I'm really wasted."

"I wouldn't fuck with you, Drew. You're too righteous. It was that same girl who walked in and out that other night. I didn't get a good look at her. I asked her name and she just said she'd come back another time."

"Wow, that's trippy."

Loren says something that I can't make out and then I hear the dial tone.

"Who were you talking to?" Emily asks. She's standing next to me.

"My friend Loren. He wanted to party."

"I didn't hear the phone ring."

"You were asleep. You were pretty out of it. You still are."

"So are you, honey. Let's go to bed."

It's really hot, even with the air conditioner running, so we lay under a single sheet.

"Whatever happens between us, Drew, I love you. I really do."

"What do you mean, whatever happens?"

"I don't know. This voice keeps telling me that we love each other but can't be together right now."

She passes out. I lay awake, the buzz rapidly depleting as paranoia sets in.

Emily doesn't remember much from the night before, so I don't grill her about her stoned epiphany. She spends the day at the condo. We make love and listen to records.

"This place could use a woman's touch," she says.

"That bad?" I ask.

"No, it's not that. It just looks so empty and lonely. Is your brother a bachelor?"

"He is now," I say. "Paul got divorced over a year ago. His ex-wife, Caroline, is an attorney. She left him for one of the partners in the firm. Messy stuff. She still lives in Boston."

"That's sad," she says. "Someone always gets hurt. Does he like Stanford? Palo Alto is beautiful."

"Yeah, he seems to. We talk every few weeks. He's coming back at the end of August."

"I wish I could move in with you here," she says.

"I don't think we could afford it. I'm not sure my brother can to tell you the truth. He got the condo as part of the divorce settlement. Caroline kind of bought him off. She makes an obscene amount of money."

"That doesn't sound so bad. I wouldn't mind being rich someday," she says. "Ryan's family is wealthy. I know it's silly to want that but I grew up kind of poor until my mom's career got going. I don't want to do that bohemian student thing much longer. How about you?"

"What do you mean?" I ask.

"You know, are you going to stay in Boston when your brother comes back?"

"I want to be wherever you are."

"You shouldn't plan your life around me, Drew. We're barely an item."

"I guess I'm not very good at planning ahead."

"What about work? You're so much better than what you're doing now. You shouldn't be temping and freelancing. You're so talented, Drew. People should know who you are. You should be the editor of NME or something."

I laugh, but it hurts to hear her words. I feel insecure listening to Emily being ambitious on my behalf. I want to tell her about the potential job with Spin, but at this point I'd rather be with her, anywhere, than be without her in New York.

"You look worried," she says. "I wasn't trying to bum you out. I just think you're really smart and cool, and that you don't give yourself enough credit. You have so many good stories to tell. You should write a book."

"Like a memoir?"

"Or maybe even a novel, but make sure to change my name if you write about me," she says with a grin.

Claire Hates Me

Emily and I spend the next few weeks in a state of feigned bliss. We hang out at Paul's condo, making love and listening to music, trying not to speak about the nooses tightening around our necks. Emily has to talk to Ryan. I have things to sort out with Claire. She keeps procrastinating, saying she'll talk to Ryan in person when he visits. I finally call Claire's dad but he doesn't pick up. I leave a message on his machine, asking if he knows where Claire is, saying I need to move on with my life. I don't mention the word divorce, but I ramble on with some authority until the machine cuts me off.

Claire phones the very next day. I almost drop my cup of coffee on the floor when I hear her voice. It's too uncanny that she's called the day after I tried to reach her father. It's like she's been psychically spying on me, secretly keeping tabs on me from the astral plane. I wonder if there was any truth to her claims of psychic powers after all. That, maybe, she really could see portals to other dimensions.

"What do you want?" I ask, trying not to sound too pissed off, before remembering that it's probably best to be civil so I can iron out the divorce once and for all.

"No need to be grumpy," says Claire. She sounds baked and distant. "I just wanted to see if you're okay."

"I am."

"How's Boston?"

"It's okay." This is feeling a little weird. We haven't spoken in months and now she's engaging in small talk.

"That's good. I'm in Bath now."

"I know. I had to find out from one of your former co-workers. She said you didn't leave a forwarding address."

"I'm sorry," she says. "I meant to tell you, but I'm not always in tune. I lose track of time on the physical plane."

I laugh.

"What's so funny?" she asks.

"You sound like you've lost your mind. What kind of Kool-Aid has Sean been feeding you?"

"That's not funny. There's no need to be hostile. Sean has been good to me. He wanted to leave Glastonbury in a hurry. He didn't like the vibes there. We're living in an old farm house in the country with friends."

"Like the Manson family?"

She goes silent before continuing. "I knew you wouldn't understand. You don't believe in a higher power. You never did. You're too negative."

"It's not that. I don't care what you believe in… it's just that damn commune thing."

"We're like a big family. Everyone's happy." Claire sounds tired. I'm not convinced.

"Sorry," I say. "This is too bizarre for me. I don't get it. I don't want to fight."

"I don't want to fight anymore either, Drew."

"Good. There are some things we need to settle."

"Like what?

"Like getting a divorce. I really need to move on, Claire."

"You've met someone, haven't you?"

"Yes."

Claire doesn't respond.

"Are you still there?" I ask.

"Yes. I'm just sad. I had a feeling you had—that's why I called."

"So why are you sad? You're allowed to move on, but I'm not?"

"I know it's not fair, but that's how I feel."

"So, basically, you don't want me to be happy."

"It's not that, it's just that I remember how much you used to love me. You used to always say, 'until the end of the world.' It makes me sad that you'll never say those words to me again."

I feel a pang of guilt before remembering that she was the one who left me.

"I really do want you to be happy," she says, "but I'm not convinced you are. Tell me about her." She puts emphasis on the word her, like she's describing an evil succubus.

Against my better judgment, I tell Claire about Emily. Probably too much.

"She's too young for you," Claire says.

"It's a smaller age gap than the one you have with that decrepit hippie," I say.

"That's not fair, Drew. I just want you to be happy, but I think you're making the wrong choice."

"Well, that's for me to find out. It's not like I'm marrying her. I just want to get divorced. I need my freedom."

"Freedom is a state of mind. Marriage is just a piece of paper. Your beliefs are too conventional to understand that, but if that's what you need, I'll sign the papers."

When I get off the phone, I sort through some CDs. I pick up one by the Lilys called *In The Presence of Nothing*. It came out a few years ago, but I only recently heard about them through an acquaintance who works at Newbury Comics. I pop it into the player and immediately enjoy the sonic rush. They're like an American take on My Bloody Valentine. As I flip through the credits, I shudder. The last track is called "Claire Hates Me."

Plaything

I speak to an attorney in Belfast the next day. He says he'll mail the paperwork for me to fill out, adding that the proceedings shouldn't be too complicated since we don't own any joint property. I try to focus on my writing. I have two interviews coming up. I'm writing a semi-extensive piece on the highly touted Liverpool band Cast for Alternative Press and a smaller article on Northern Ireland's Ash for Spin. Nick is a big Ash fan. He told me the Belfast trio reminds him of all the seventies punk acts he grew up with. I listen to the Cast and Ash records and try to prep for the interviews, but I keep daydreaming about Emily instead. Now that I've started divorce proceedings, I feel like a huge weight has been lifted off my shoulders, that I can finally exorcise Claire's ghost.

I tell Emily about Claire's call. She seems happy for me, but not as much as I'd hoped. She still hasn't talked to Ryan and seems uncomfortable when I quiz her about it.

"I'm so scared about how Ryan's going to react," she said. "When we talk on the phone he keeps talking about our future, but all I can think about is you. I need to be as brave as you were with Claire and just move on."

That was on Sunday night. I phoned her on Monday and she didn't answer. I left another message on Tuesday. Still no answer. She finally returned my call on Wednesday.

"I'm sorry I didn't get back to you sooner," she says. "I've been frantic because Ryan's visiting tomorrow and I still don't know what to do."

"The right words will come," I say. "You just have to be honest." I grimace to myself on the inside. One cliché after another, but what else can I say? I'm a little pissed off that it was so easy for me to talk to Claire, but Emily's still pussyfooting with Ryan. I feel better when she says that she wants to see me before the Cast show, before she has to meet Ryan.

Cast are playing at The Paradise. It's my favorite concert venue in Boston. A vast room with a balcony and great acoustics. Earlier in the day I get a haircut. Nothing drastic, just a small trim. I brought in a picture of Keith Richards from 1966 as an example. The girl who cut it did a nice job. I want to look my best for Emily, especially since she's about to dump another guy for me. I'm wearing a short sleeve Ben Sherman, black jeans, Chelsea boots, and shades. I feel cool on the outside, queasy on the inside.

I have a brief chat with Cast's singer, John Powers. He's friendly, super baked, and easy to talk to. I let the recorder do the work as John tells me about music's mystical healing powers. I tell him about seeing Lou Reed and tearing up during "Rock and Roll."

"See what I mean, la," says John. "Rock 'n' roll is fookin' magic."

After the interview I go to the Thai restaurant next door and order a Rolling Rock at the bar. I have fifteen minutes to kill before Emily is due to arrive. I flip through the latest issue of Select, which I stuffed into my backpack with my tape recorder. Last summer the British press couldn't get enough about the battle between Blur and Oasis. Now that Oasis have been declared the victors, there's a spread about new bands who might follow in Oasis' footsteps. Noelrock, they're calling it. I notice a photo of Northern Uproar, the band Dave was working with.

Emily taps me on the shoulder. She looks like she's seen a ghost. She sits next to me.

"So what's up?" I ask. My spider sense is telling me that Emily isn't a bearer of good news.

"There's something I haven't told you." She looks upset, like she might cry.

"Good or bad?" I ask, knowing full well it's the latter.

"You're going to be mad."

"Okay." I can feel my stomach turn.

"Last month I got a job offer to write for an alternative weekly in San Francisco. That was just before we saw Electrafixion, before you know…"

Yeah, I know, Emily, before we fucked I say to myself. "So, I'm guessing you're going to take the job?"

"I have to."

"That's okay," I say. "I'll come with you. There's nothing keeping me here."

"It's not that easy," she says.

"You're not breaking up with him, are you?" I feel like Watson in one of his dumber moments, before he sees the light.

"No," she says. She avoids eye contact and looks down on the floor. Some things never change. Emily always looks at the floor when the subject is Ryan.

"So, was I just a whirlwind fling because you were having mommy issues?"

I'm shaking and my stomach is hurting. I can feel tears well up inside.

"That's not fair," she says. "I care about you more than you'll ever know. It just wouldn't work out. I know it. Ryan called last night after I talked to you. I told him everything. He still wants to be with me. He even blamed himself for being away. I know he's not perfect, but I owe it to him to give him another chance."

I think about Loren's words. Those young girls will be into you one minute and drop you without rhyme or reason the next. Something to that effect. I order a shot. Emily doesn't leave.

"You don't have to stay," I say. "It's clear you don't want to."

She starts crying and I take her hand.

"Don't hate me," she says. "What would you do if Claire called you again and said it was all a mistake, that she wants you back? Would you forgive her? Would you take her back despite your feelings for me?"

I pause, trying to find the right words. "No," I finally say. "I'd like to think that she's scarred me far too much to take her back. I love you Emily."

"I know you love me, Drew. Your passion is real. No one has wanted me like you do. I'm going to miss that part…"

"It doesn't have to end," I say. "Let's go away somewhere, right now. We'll just start driving."

Maybe it's the alcohol but I feel reckless, like I'm the lead player in a doomed road movie, knowing full well I'll meet certain death at the border, but unafraid to see my mission through.

There's a trace of a smile on Emily's face. "You're too much of a dreamer, Drew," she says. "I love that about you, but I know someday I might not find that part of you so endearing. You're too much like my dad. I don't want to end up like my parents."

She squeezes my hand and gives me a quick kiss on the lips before she leaves.

I don't know why I go to the concert but I do. I torture myself by watching the show from the balcony where I can see Emily and Ryan down below, cavorting near the stage. Their body language is that of a couple on a first date. Hesitant, occasionally holding hands, but awkward. Losing trust in someone does that to you. I've been on the receiving end several times. Most of us have. Ryan was a prick at the Velvet Crush show, and nothing Emily's said about him since has made me like him more. I wish I could feel sorry for him, but I don't. He's an asshole, who's going to become a wealthy asshole and no doubt spawn wealthy asshole kids, who will be awarded with legacy admissions to Harvard as long as he donates enough bread to the old alma matter. I watch them from above like a cruel voyeur, the phantom of the Britpop opera.

Cast are good though they have a tendency to jam too much, like they're headlining a hippie festival. I don't really need to hear extended versions of what are more or less carbon copies of sixties Who songs. I think about leaving until they play "Walkaway." This was Emily's favorite, and I liked it, too. It's a sad, defiant ballad about knowing when it's over and when to move on. Power's sweet melody and soaring chorus, which repeats the words 'walk away' several times in a lilting Scouse accent, brought a tear to my eye when I was happily hanging out in the apartment with Emily. Hearing it in this setting, just hours after the bomb dropped—the girl responsible standing below me—is far too painful. I look over the railing and see Emily walk toward the front door. I wonder if she's thinking the same thing. I follow her outside.

I find her leaning against a wall, smoking a cigarette, hands visibly shaking.

"Hey you," she says, her voice far less sultry than her greeting ten weeks ago at the Lush concert. She sounds sad and exhausted.

"Hey you," I say. "What's with the cigarette?"

"I bummed one from Ryan. He smokes. I only smoke when I'm sad. I had to go outside when 'Walkaway' came on. It made me think about you."

"And here I am, but I'm leaving."

"Goodbye, Drew."

"Goodbye, Emily."

I walk away, that damn Cast song stuck in my head. I want to turn around and look at her one last time, but my pride gets in the way and I forge on. Don't look back in anger, as Oasis said.

I arrive home hot and sweaty. I take a cold shower, liberate a beer from the refrigerator, and put on a cassette compilation I made of Whipping Boy B-Sides culled from their UK singles. These songs are darker than the material on *Heartworm*, and suits my present mood just fine.

"Plaything" comes on. Emily didn't like it. "It reminds me too much of us," she once said.

"Do you remember the little things we did as I lay with

you and you had no regrets?" Fearghal asks when the song kicks in. "I've listened to your lines. I've listened to your lies. I've listened to you too much and you buried me inside." The chorus is brutal and angst-ridden: "I belong to you and you belong to me. I belong to you and you belong to another man."

I turn off the tape and go to the Red Dragon. Loren's at the bar talking to Jethro. A couple of old drunks, who I've never seen before, are sitting in one of the booths. I realize that I've never seen a woman here. I remember the weird phone conversation I had with Loren about the girl who was looking for me. I haven't been back since. There wasn't any reason to while I was with Emily.

Jethro hands me a beer.

"You look bummed out buddy," he says. "This one's on the house."

"Thanks, man."

Jethro doesn't say anything else and leaves the bar to collect stray bottles and glasses. He's not big on conversation unless he's high and the subject matter is movies, in particular, his beloved westerns.

I tell Loren about Emily.

"Dude, I'm hurting for you," he says. "I know I can be cynical as all fuck, but I was in your corner. It's cold how she just dropped you. I thought you had something more. Did you guys ever talk about the future?"

"Not much. She did tell me that I should be doing a lot more with my life. It was just a short conversation."

"That was the interview," says Loren. "You didn't get the job."

"What do you mean?" I ask, taken aback.

"I don't mean to be so cold, brother, but she sat down and did the math. A dude who goes to Stanford law school is a safe bet. All the things she liked about you, like being slack and mellow…"

"And being good in bed," I say with a forced smile.

"That too," Loren says. He laughs and we bump fists before he continues. "I'm sure she dug your mysterious side, but it probably scared her. Chicks want certainty. They don't embrace the desperado lifestyle."

"Desperado?" asks Jethro. He's back at the bar, half paying attention. "Are we talking about cowboy flicks?"

"Nah," says Loren. "Just chicks."

Jethro leaves to lock the front door.

"You guys want to get high?" he asks. "I've got a special blend"

"Sure," says Loren.

"Sure," I say. "What's so special about this blend, Jethro?"

"Ancient Chinese secret," says Jethro.

When I wake up, I'm still at the Red Dragon. I can't figure out what time it is. I feel groggy. Jethro's behind the bar and Loren is still next to me on my right. Claire is seated to my left.

"Hi, Drew," she says. "It's been a long time."

I must be dreaming. I try to wake up. I can't. I try to scream my way awake. I still can't. Everyone is laughing.

"Where am I?" I ask. "Did I die?"

"You're in limbo, but you're just visiting," says Claire. Her gorgeous red hair is longer than ever, well past her shoulders. She's ghostly pale.

Loren and Jethro walk away to one of the booths. "You guys need time to talk," says Loren.

I gaze into Claire's eyes. "So I'm not dead? What about Jethro and Loren."

She looks down at the bar. "They're dead, Drew. They're lost souls who need to make peace with themselves before they can move on."

"Are you dead?" I ask.

"No," she says. "I came here to find you. I've been watching you for a while. You know I can do that sort of thing."

"I know," I say. Portals for Claire. Portholes for Bono.

I try to wake up. I still can't. I decide I don't need to.

"You won't wake up until you're ready," says Claire, reading my thoughts.

"Will I see you again?" I ask. "I mean, will I see you in the real world?"

"Yes," she says.

We sit there in silence for what feels like an eternity. She takes my hand and I feel a surge of energy. She's replenishing my soul, I think. Everything feels good and pure. I don't ask her about Sean and I don't seek forgiveness for the bad things I've done. The past doesn't seem to matter anymore, at least not in this moment. My love for Claire is so strong that my heart starts to hurt. I float away, watching myself and Claire down below. Then darkness sets in.

Girl From Mars

I finally wake up. I'm in the apartment. There are several angry phone messages from my boss at Harvard, wondering why I haven't come into work, or at least called to offer a reasonable explanation. I realize that I must have slept—tripped—through an entire day and that it's now Saturday morning.

I make some coffee and sit on a chair on the balcony outside, soaking in the summer sun. When I finish my cup, I go inside to get a refill. The phone rings. It's Claire's father, Gordon.

"Sorry, I didn't return your message, Drew," he says. He sounds stern.

"That's okay. Claire called me. She let me know she's in Bath…"

"She's back in Belfast, Drew. That's why I'm phoning."

"Well, it would have been nice of her to tell me that," I say. "I just contacted an attorney. He's sending me divorce papers. I guess I'll just forward them to you." The oneness I felt with Claire in my vision has faded. She's deceived me once again. I wonder if she's brought Sean with her.

"Look, Drew," says Gordon, sounding angry. "This isn't the time to discuss those matters. Claire's very ill. She tried to kill herself. She'll be in the hospital for several weeks."

"Christ, I'm sorry." My heart is racing and I feel sick to the stomach. "What happened?"

He tells me Claire returned to Belfast a week ago, showing up on his doorstep looking pale and disheveled. "She wouldn't say much other than a friend bought her a train ticket to Wales, from where she took the ferry to Belfast. Claire was afraid and begged me not to let Sean find her. I phoned the police in Bath and they said they would look into it. They said that neighbors had filed complaints in the past, but that there was no evidence of foul play."

I tell Gordon about my last conversation with Claire, how she sounded robotic. "I've always hated Sean, but this time I want to kill him." My hand is shaking and tears are welling up.

"I should have told you she was back, but I was too shocked to do anything. She would barely eat, barely speak, and now this…"

Gordon composes himself. Like most men I've met from Northern Ireland, Gordon isn't emotional. He takes a deep breath and tells me how he found Claire in a comatose state on her bedroom floor, a bottle of sleeping pills to her side.

"Fortunately, the medics were able to get her to vomit. Otherwise she might not have made it."

"Jesus. Is she in good hands now?"

"Yes. They've assigned her a therapist. They'll be monitoring her for a while. Hopefully we'll find out more. What happened between you and Claire, Drew? She was so vulnerable after Ann passed away. I wish you could have done more to help her."

I don't like it that Gordon is blaming me. I feel guilty enough for not picking up on signs, until it was too late, that Claire had become seriously depressed after her mother's death. Never mind that a year later she'd become crazy enough to try to kill herself.

"That's not fair," I say. "I begged Claire to come to America with me. I even tried to reach out to her again when I came here."

"I'm sorry, Drew. I suppose you're right. I've always liked you. You were good to her. It was a bitter pill to swallow learning that she had run off with another man. I've lost my wife and now I've nearly lost my daughter. She may never get her back to where she was." He's very choked up.

"I'm sorry," I say. "I really am."

"She mentioned you this morning," he says.

"What did she say?"

"She woke up from a long sleep and told me you were sad, that your soul was in isolation. I know that sounds like mumbo jumbo—God knows what crazy ideas her head's filled with—but I suppose it's a good sign that she remembers something."

I don't tell Gordon about my drug-induced trip to limbo, where I visited his daughter.

"I need to see Claire," I say. Genuine concern has replaced the hurt and jealousy.

"I don't think that's a good idea," says Gordon. "They want to keep her in hospital for the rest of the month, and when she does come home, she's still going to need a lot of treatment."

"Please," I say.

"Let me talk to the doctors," he finally responds.

Even though I slept all day Friday, I feel exhausted, like I'm in detox. I crash for another fifteen hours, rising early on Sunday afternoon, and finally feeling like my old self. I go for a long walk, before remembering I have to interview Ash in a few hours.

The Ash gig is at The Paradise and the interview goes well. I chat with the singer Tim Wheeler, who's only nineteen. His lyrics show a maturity rarely realized by writers so young. Not too many kids can write about love and loss so freshly as Wheeler does on classics like "Goldfinger" and "Girl From Mars." When I tell him this, he dismisses it, like he's just singing about what's real to him. He opens up when I tell him I've been to Belfast and I'm visiting again soon. We end up talking about Ireland and bands from the north like the Undertones and Stiff Little Fingers.

The gig is amazing. I feel like every Irish expat in Boston under the age of thirty is in attendance, singing along. For a few hours I forget that just a few days ago I walked out of the Cast gig at this very same venue, holding back tears. I still can't think of Emily without choking up and now I have Claire to deal with. Just when I thought my divorce would get finalized, Claire literally turns up from the dead.

Gordon phones the next week and asks if I can visit in August. Claire will be home from the hospital by then. "She seems to get a little better every day," he says, "but she has a long way to go. She's on a lot of medication and gets easily confused."

I decide to do the following things:

　　1) Quit my job at Harvard.

　　2) Give my stash of ancient Chinese secret weed to my stoner co-worker Doug.

3) Purchase a one way ticket to Dublin with a connecting train to Belfast.

4) Let my brother know I'm leaving and that I won't be there when he comes back to Cambridge at the end of the month.

Paul's not too thrilled that I'm leaving. He's a Political Science professor, a logical and level-headed guy. "You need to move forward with your life, Drew," he says. "I know you don't feel like it, but you're doing okay. You have a job—it may not be the best job in the world—but you're working and being responsible. Your writing seems to be going well, too."

"I need to see this through," I say. "I need to see Claire even if it's for the last time."

"I feel for you, Drew. My break up with Caroline was terrible. I know what you're going through. I sympathize, but you and Claire have been separated for over a year. The odds are stacked against you. Just get the papers signed and leave it at that. It sucks that she's not well—that she tried to kill herself—but that's not your fault."

"You're probably right," I say, "but sometimes you just have to keep on driving even when you know you're headed for a cliff."

On the Aer Lingus flight I'm seated next to a young girl who's going to Trinity for junior year abroad. She's an English major at Tufts and will be taking literature courses. It crosses my mind that Claire could have been one of her instructors had she not dropped out of school. I tell her that I used to live in Ireland and she grills me for several hours, the two of us knocking back several bottles of airplane wine. She asks what I do for a living and I tell her I'm a music writer. She says that she loves U2 and the Cranberries and asks if I've ever met Bono.

"Sort of," I answer. "I've seen him raking his leaves in leather pants and once I saw him smoking cigarettes with Shane McGowan."

She laughs at my stories. I tell her that she needs to listen to Whipping Boy, that they're the best band in Ireland. She removes a small notebook from her purse. The word *Heartworm* looks funny in girlish handwriting on pink paper. Soon after she nods off, but I can't sleep. I wish I had a Valium. Right now I just want to sink into emptiness. Let sleep come down and kill the bad dreams. Kill the memories of Claire. Kill the affair with Emily. Kill my rock 'n' roll dreams and start all over again. Year Zero. I look out the window. It's too dark to see the Atlantic, but I catch glimpses of stars. They don't inspire hope. The view is ominous. I wonder if my porthole would inspire more positive words from Bono, maybe something about saving the indigenous people in Greenland.

I arrive in Belfast mid-day. Gordon greets me at the door. He looks rough, as if he's aged ten years in the last two. I can understand that. He's now fully gray and I notice wrinkles that I never saw before. Between his wife's death and his daughter's meltdown, I don't know how he copes. Gordon's normally stern and serious—the stiff handshake type—but this time he hugs me and tells me that he's happy to see me. I say likewise.

"Claire's taking a nap," he says. "She's tired all the time, but it's better than when she was first admitted to the hospital. She was having horrible nightmares then and screaming a lot. It was terrible."

"I'm here to help," I say. "I'll do all I can."

"I appreciate that. But don't get your hopes up."

I take my suitcase to the guest room and lie back in bed, the exhaustion from the flight and train catching up to me. It feels like I've slept for hours, but when I look at the clock on the nightstand I see that it's only 8:00. I hear voices downstairs. Claire's awake.

I go to the dining room. Claire and Gordon are drinking tea. Claire smiles and looks at me with a quizzical expression.

"You remember Drew, don't you?" asks Gordon.

"Yes," she finally says in an almost robotic tone. "Hi Drew."

Claire's hair is long, well past her shoulders, just as it was in my vision. She's terribly thin, almost anorexic. She rises slowly—it seems difficult for her just to get up. She hugs me for what feels like the longest time, occasionally touching my hair. It's like she's searching for some spark of memory.

"Why don't you let Drew sit down," says Gordon. "Would you like some tea, Drew?"

"Sure," I say.

"Drew prefers coffee," says Claire.

Gordon and I laugh. It feels like a good omen.

"Tea's okay," I say. I pour myself a cup, dumping in several teaspoons of sugar.

"I ordered Chinese takeout," says Gordon. "I was going to pick it up now. Are you okay watching Claire for a little while?" It feels like he's asking me to babysit.

"Sure," I say.

"Drew likes music, doesn't he, da?"

"Yes," says Gordon.

"Do you want to listen to a record, Drew?"

"Sure," I say.

Claire takes my hand and leads me to her bedroom. The walk upstairs tires her out. She stands for a good minute at the top of the stairs, catching her breath. Her bedroom is like a time capsule. Nothing has changed since Claire was eighteen, when she left for university. There are posters on the wall of Duran Duran, the Smiths, Echo and the Bunnymen, plus a funny one of U2 when they were really young. Bono's wearing ridiculous boots with huge Cuban heels, the Edge is cradling his guitar like a baby, Adam poses like a seventies rock star with his out-of-control white boy afro, while baby-faced Larry sheepishly stares off into space.

Claire carefully places Duran Duran's "Girls on Film" on her ancient turntable and giggles. This record came out when Claire was sixteen and it's all starting to make sense. Claire has regressed to her teenage self and she's reliving her youthful crush on John Taylor. I'm scared to know what kind of trauma reduced Claire to this state, but right now she's happy, dopey, and medicated. Next she puts on *Kilimanjaro*.

"Do you like the Teardrop Explodes?" she asks.

I say I do. She's sitting back in bed, her head bobbing along to the psychedelic grooves and Julian Cope's whimsical lyrics. I'm seated on the floor, thumbing through her collection, smiling, happy in the moment. Gordon returns as "Brave Boys Keep Their Promises" is spinning. I think about promises I never kept, all the people I've let down. Chinese food, even Chinese food made in Belfast, is a welcome relief from my demons.

The next day Claire has an appointment at the hospital, followed by a session with the psychologist she sees twice a week. The doctors seem happy with Claire's progress. She's slowly putting on weight and her vital signs are better. What the shrink thinks is anyone's guess. Gordon and I have a cup of coffee during Claire's session.

He asks me point blank if there's anyone else in my life, if I've moved on.

I say no, telling him there was someone briefly, but that it didn't work out. I don't know why I apologize but I do.

"There's no need to be sorry, Drew," says Gordon. "It's been more than a year since Claire left you. I would have expected you to try to move on at some point."

"It's hard," I say.

"I know," he says. "It's nearly two years since Ann passed and I still have a hard time. Friends have been trying to set me up on dates, but I don't feel ready, especially now with Claire in so much trouble. Worrying about her and my job is more than enough. Classes start next month and I don't know what I'll do with Claire. You can't stay here forever…"

"I wish I could go back in time and fix what went wrong with Claire. We started to drift apart, even before Ann died. I don't know if we could ever be together again, but I need to know that she'll be okay, that she's in good hands."

Over the following fortnight, I spend more time with Claire, taking her to appointments and to her favorite record store, Good Vibrations, which is owned by Terri Hooley. He's the man who discovered the Undertones and brought punk rock to Northern Ireland. Claire seems confused by CDs, and heads straight to the vinyl section, thumbing through releases by her favorite eighties bands. She pulls out *Hatful of Hollow* and says, "This was my favorite record when I first went to university. I studied in England."

I don't respond, shocked—but happy—that a Smiths record of all things has triggered a memory.

"Yes, you did," I finally say. "You were at Essex in Colchester."

She smiles. It seems forced, as if she's struggling to remember more. I don't press her, don't tell her that we met there. She seems comfortable with me, like I'm an old friend. Part of me doesn't want her to know that we fell in love and fell apart, even though I know someday she has to if she's to heal.

"Can I get an ice cream?" she asks. She's back to acting like my kid sister. We find a stand that sells 99's—soft serve vanilla with a Cadbury's flake inserted inside—and sit on a park bench, taking in a brief blast of Belfast sun. When it clouds up, I tell her it's time to go home.

A few days later, we're in her room and she puts on *Psychocandy*.

"Do you remember when we saw them at Norwich University, Drew?" she asks.

"Yes," I say.

"That's when I knew I liked you, but you liked Julie then."

"But I ended up liking you a lot more," I say.

Claire smiles. When *Psychocandy* finishes, she cues up an old Human League 45, "Don't You Want Me." I wonder if the Jesus and Mary Chain memory has already subsided. I think she's settled back into her sixteen-year-old headspace. Then I remember.

"We danced to this song together, once, Drew, at a pub in Clacton. That's when I knew you liked me as much as I liked you."

"I remember," I say.

She takes my hand and kisses me. I'm too startled to respond.

"You can kiss me back, silly," she says. "You're my boyfriend."

I kiss her softly and tell her it's time for her pills.

"I don't like pills," she says. "I can't feel anything when I take them."

"What do you mean?"

"I feel like a robot. I'm never happy and I'm never sad."

"You need to take them until you get better. I don't want you to be sad." I say.

"When will I get better?" she asks. "I want to feel something." She starts to cry. I hold her.

"It's so frustrating," she says. "I can't hold on to things. I can't remember why I love you, but I know I do."

The next day Gordon takes Claire to her appointments.

"Why don't you give yourself the day off, Drew," he says. "I know how much you like Belfast. You haven't had much time to yourself the last few weeks."

I walk to Good Vibrations and decide to buy Claire some records. Her collection at her father's house ends in 1986. We bought everything together after that. If *Psychocandy* could trigger happy memories, maybe some newer records will have a similar effect. I go to the ever dwindling vinyl section—a sign of the digital times, even in a store as cool as Good Vibrations—and purchase copies of *Achtung Baby*, the Stone Roses' self-titled debut, and *Honey's Dead*. Claire loved all of these records at one time in her life. I smile remembering Emily stripping to *Honey's Dead* in my bedroom. It feels so long ago now. I'm not mad at her anymore. I also find a copy of *Heartworm* on blue vinyl, a cool collector's item. I decide that I won't share this record with Claire just yet. The memories associated with *Heartworm* are all mine, and they're sad and nostalgic, mostly because of her. It's my secret, my shrink.

On the way home I take a detour into West Belfast. IRA country. It's a dangerous neighborhood if you're a Protestant, but as a lapsed American Catholic, I feel reasonably safe. Claire once scolded me for going there.

"Why would you want to visit somewhere where I'm not welcome?" she asked.

I had been reading up on the Troubles and become enamored with the story of the hunger strikers, the young men who starved themselves in prison, fighting for the right to be reclassified as political prisoners. I was sixteen when this happened and I remember listening to updates on National Public Radio every morning as I'd get ready for school. The most famous hunger striker, Bobby Sands, apparently used to be a runner, so some of the distance runners at my school and I started referring to ourselves as the Bobby Sands Track Club. Part of it, admittedly, was sick schoolboy humor—we were all rail thin—but we also meant it as a form of tribute. My political leanings and those of my friends were strongly left of center as we raged against injustices in places like South Africa, Nicaragua, El Salvador, and Ireland.

West Belfast is full of fascinating political murals. Buildings are elaborately painted with homages to the struggle—historical figures like the heroes of the 1916 Easter Rising and more recent icons like Sands and fellow striker Joe McDonnell. There are also terrifying images of balaclava masked men, waving AK-47s in defiance of the British government and Protestant vigilante gangs. I'm gazing at a portrait of Bobby Sands and Che Guevara—the IRA consider themselves to be revolutionary socialists and have links to the PLO and Basque freedom fighters—when a young boy approaches me. He's dressed in a track suit and trainers, standard working-class casual garb.

"What are you looking at?" he asks, not so politely.

I tell him that I'm a writer, that I'm interested in Irish history.

"Are you Catholic or Protestant?" he asks.

"I'm an American," I say.

"Yes, but are you an American Catholic or an American Protestant?"

"I'm a Catholic," I say, a little saddened by the boy's need to question. I wonder if he ever attended a Cooperation North workshop.

"That's good," he says. "I thought as much. You'd have to be fookin' mad to come here if you weren't."

He asks if I have any spare change, so I hand him a fiver and he dashes off, content in the moment. I consider exploring the Protestant neighborhoods in the Shankhill, but decide not to. My mood has soured. The murals there are even more violent and threatening than the ones in West Belfast, one of them even honoring Michael Stone, a man who killed three innocent Catholic mourners at a Republican funeral. In contrast to the violent imagery, the neighborhood itself is meticulously neat and clean, the curbsides carefully detailed in red, white, and blue paint in tribute to the Union Jack. More British than the rest of Britain.

Claire and Gordon are having tea when I return.

"I bought you some records, Claire," I say.

She smiles. "What did you buy?" she asks.

"I'll show you when we finish our tea," I say, feeling like a father at Christmas, telling his daughter she has to wait to open her presents.

I can't get a good read on Gordon's expression. A few days earlier he seemed skeptical when I told him that I thought music was helping Claire's recovery.

"It's going to take a lot more than that, Drew," he said. "Therapy is the answer. I appreciate what you're doing, but don't get your hopes up."

Gordon offered me some advice. "You can't put your life on hold much longer, Drew. Claire's not going to be better overnight."

"What do you suggest then?" I asked, not really wanting to hear his answer.

"I think you should get divorced. I think we should sort things out before you leave."

"That's pretty cold." I guessed that I had worn out my welcome.

"I'm just being realistic, Drew. You and Claire separated for a reason, you can't let nostalgia get in the way. You both need to move on."

"Despite everything that happened to us, she's still my wife." I struggled to get the words out, knowing on some level he was right.

"I know, Drew. I know you want to do what's best. I see how you act around her... We don't have to talk about this anymore today, but it needs to be addressed."

Until The End of The World

Claire's U2 collection stopped at *The Unforgettable Fire*, but I feel that there'll be no harm done if she bypasses *The Joshua Tree* and *Rattle and Hum* and goes straight to *Achtung Baby*. Claire seems to like it. I was hoping "Until the End of the World" would register with her, that she would remember our inside joke, but she just nods along, reacting no differently to anything else on the album.

"Is this a new record?" she asks. "I don't remember it."

"It's fairly new," I say, not wanting to tell her it came out five years ago.

"I like it, but I like this one better," she says reaching for her copy of Lloyd Cole and the Commotions *Rattlesnakes*. "We used to listen to this a lot, didn't we?"

"Yes," I say. She kisses me again, like she did the other night. I'm nervous, but also turned on. I know my feelings are inappropriate, but I can't help it. It's simple biology. I feel myself transported to the small room at Essex where we fell in love when we were young. I kiss her back. She's too distracted to continue. She gets up and hands me a coffee table book about Ireland. We sit there on her bed, slowly thumbing through the section about Giant's Causeway. It's a breathtaking site, consisting of spectacular rock formations on the northeast coast of Ireland.

"I used to go there when I was a child," she says. "We went there once, too."

"We did. It was a nice trip." Claire and I went there for our honeymoon, spending a few days at a nearby B&B, doing nothing but taking long walks in the afternoon and making love in the evening. We joked that we would retire there when we got old.

"Can we go again?" she asks.

I say I'll talk to her dad. Gordon is reluctant, but I promise that it will be a day trip and that I'll have her home by dinner time.

The next day Claire goes shopping with an old school friend and gets her hair and nails done. When she comes back, I hardly recognize her. Her hair is cut short in a stylish bob, almost exactly like it was when we first met.

"What do you think, Drew?" she asks.

I tell her I love it though I'm freaked out that she looks like she did when we first fell in love. She smiles. Gordon asks what she bought, noticing a shopping bag from Miss Selfridge on the floor. Claire pulls out a black dress.

"It's for tomorrow," she says. "When we go to the cemetery. It will be two years since mum died. We should bring her some flowers."

Gordon turns pale, shocked that Claire is able to remember the painful anniversary. Ann's death had been a taboo subject around the house.

The trip to the cemetery isn't as dramatic as I feared. Gordon seems extremely relieved, too. He's been less optimistic about Claire's recovery than I have. Whenever I comment about her progress, Gordon contradicts me, bringing up potential scenarios that the doctors warned him about. Claire is quiet and cries a lot. Hopefully it's therapeutic.

Claire couldn't accept that her mother was gone when she first died. She kept telling me that she could communicate with Ann from beyond the grave. The idiots at the healing center in Sandymount, particularly Sean, fed on her vulnerability. Now it feels like there's some closure. In the early hours of the morning, Claire sneaks into my bed. She doesn't say anything. She just gets under the covers and holds me. When I wake up she's gone. I wonder if it was a dream.

When I go downstairs, Claire is already dressed, hurrying me to get ready so we can visit the Giant's Causeway. She doesn't say anything about being in my bed. The first leg of the journey is a train ride to the town of Coleraine, about an hour northwest of Belfast. Claire sits next to me, never letting go of my hand. Just when I think she's reverting back to small child mode, she surprises me.

"Bad things happened to me when I left Dublin, Drew. I'm starting to remember things in therapy."

"I'm sorry. I should have been a better husband after Ann died." Guilty memories of my friendship with Siobhan come back.

"Sean made us do bad things."

"Made who do bad things?" I ask.

"The other girls who lived with us. He told the other men to share their wives and girlfriends with him. He said was empowering them with his knowledge."

She starts to cry. I'm too shocked and appalled to say anything. This is crazy Jim Jones shit.

"I don't remember taking the pills," she says. "I know you've been wondering about that. Dr. Stewart has been helping me with hypnotherapy. She also thinks you should go home. She says you're an unnecessary distraction."

Part of me knows that's true, but another part wonders if Claire's just traded in one guru for another. Her head-shrinker and Sean might differ, but the end results are similar.

"Do you want me to leave? Am I an unnecessary distraction?"

"I like having you here," she says, "I wish we could go back in time. Is that possible?"

"I don't know," I say after a long pause.

"I don't know either," she says. "It makes me sad."

The train rolls into Coleraine and we have a half hour to kill before we board a bus to Bushmills, further to the north. We have a cup of tea in the station café and sit across from each other, not saying anything. She's crying and I'm too paralyzed to think straight. On the bus I hold her hand and tell her that whatever happens, I'll always love her. She smiles and asks, "Until the end of the world?" and I cry. The two of us must be an amusing sight.

From Bushmills we take another bus to the Giant's Causeway, which is situated on the tip of Northern Ireland. We have a quick lunch at the pub at the Causeway Hotel, where I sink a much needed pint of Guinness, before we proceed down a steep path that leads to the glorious basalt columns, the result of an ancient volcanic eruption, or a confrontation between the Irish giant Finn MacCool and his Scottish rival Benandonner, should you choose to believe the legend. The winds are picking up, causing the waves from the Irish Sea to crash into the rocks on shore with extreme force. It begins to rain, and Bono jokes aside, it's starting to feel like the end of the world.

Claire has gone quiet. We're standing on top of one of the smaller columns, looking out to sea. The rain's coming down hard now and we don't have an umbrella. I ask Claire if she wants to go back to the pub to warm up, but she doesn't say anything. She squeezes my hand and looks off into space. She's lost and I don't know how to help her. At this moment I realize she might never recover. Is she going to need her father's full-time care forever? What will happen when he dies? I feel overwhelmed and out of my element. I start to cry. The rain shields my tears and Claire doesn't notice my discomfort. I tell her I love her. This time she says nothing. She just looks at me with blank, hollow eyes. I'm back to being a stranger.

In the middle of the night Claire screams. I run out to the hall. Gordon is already there, holding her, trying to get her to calm her. She's bleeding. I see gashes on her left arm. There's blood on her nightdress and all over Gordon's T-shirt.

"Jesus," I say.

Gordon glares at me like I'm a fly on the windscreen that he wants to smash. "Damn it. Grab a towel, Drew. I've called an ambulance."

Gordon and I sit with Claire in the back, the medic tending to her wounds. Claire mutters that she wanted to feel something. The emergency doctor tells us that the cuts aren't very deep. He describes it as a cry for attention, rather than a suicide attempt, though he seems alarmed to learn it's her second attempt in two months.

"We've sedated her and she's resting now," says the doctor. "She wasn't making much sense. She kept saying something about the end of the world."

"It's that bloody cult she was in," says Gordon.

He's wrong this time, but I don't tell. I sense that Claire was just trying to say goodbye to me, however violent and dramatic the means. I knew at the Causeway it was over, but I didn't know she was so torn up inside. I thought she hated me when she left, not understanding that love isn't a light switch that can be turned on and off on a whim.

Gordon and I meet with Claire's shrink the next day. She says it's probably best I leave. She tries to assure me that it's not my fault, but tells me that my presence is distracting Claire, not helping her move forward with her life. Gordon concurs almost too enthusiastically.

The last time I saw Claire she was sitting up in her hospital bed, smiling and reading a music magazine. Despite what she had gone through, she looked young that day, the way she looked when we first met. I held her hand and told her that it was time for me to go home.

"Will I see you again?" she asked.

"Yes," I lied, holding back tears. "I love you."

"Until the end of the world?"

Morning Rise

I book a return flight from Dublin to Boston that will depart in a few days. I've worn out my welcome in Belfast. I feel certain that Gordon is glad to see the back of me, though he does thank me profusely for trying to help. The key word is try. The sight of Claire's sliced-up arms will be imprinted in my mind forever. I feel rotten about leaving her behind in such a state, but her latest act of defiance made it clear that she isn't ready to get better anytime soon. I listen to *Heartworm* on the train to Dublin and the ballad "Morning Rise" prophecies, "when our time comes, I will know."

I arrive at Connolly Station in the early evening and weave my way through the worker bees escaping the city to their suburban enclaves. I decide to walk to the hotel. I navigate my way across the O'Connell Bridge, briefly gazing down on the Liffey River below, the dividing point for north and south Dublin. I'm staying at the Clarence, which is owned by U2, the Dublin equivalent of London's Columbia, if you will. It's located in the trendy Temple Bar district of the city, a haven for foreign tourists and rowdy locals. Despite the leisurely stroll, my heart is racing, as though I'm in the final stages of a Tour de France hill climb. I think I'm going to have a panic attack any second. Belfast feels like a bad dream, like none of it could have possibly happened. Claire said she wanted to feel something, anything, but at this moment, I don't want to feel a damn thing. I want to be comatose, comfortably numb. What do I even have to live for? A fucking spare bedroom in Boston?

I check into my room and lie back in bed, staring at the cracks in the ceiling. I think about Claire. Despite how horrific the incident was and how fucked up she must be inside, the bottom line is that she still wanted to live. She would have cut herself more deeply, and not woken us up, had she really wanted to die. Like the doctor said, it was a big cry for attention. All she wanted to do was feel something, anything. I stew over one of Fearghal's lyrics: "Five stories high, five ways to die. Machete, gun, flick-knife, boot and needle passed from dangerous lovers to each other." Which method would I choose?

A high-school classmate died of carbon monoxide poisoning inside his parents' garage. His mother discovered him slumped over the steering wheel, the engine still running. At the time I couldn't understand why he wanted to take his life. He was a bright kid who had just been admitted to a good college, but depression isn't a choice. Some of us are just wired that way. I think of my friend Damien who died from a heroin overdose.

Damien and I met when I first came to Dublin in '86. He was my age and a regular at the bar I worked at. He told me that he was a DJ; that he spun at a place called the Underground, a now legendary club where my favorite bands like Whipping Boy and Into Paradise first cut their teeth. Claire and I came out to see him spin a few times and we became friends. Damien was pale and frail; a gentle soul. His mannerisms reminded me a little of Plato, James Dean's sidekick, played by Sal Mineo, in *Rebel Without a Cause*. At the time a smack epidemic was rampant in Dublin, but I would have never expected Damien to have been a user. He seemed too happy and well adjusted for anything so extreme. The last time I saw him, he let me finish his DJ set. He said that he wanted to have a quiet pint, that he trusted his records in my hands. The following day I got a call from a mutual friend, telling me that Damien was dead. He was discovered in the back of his car behind a suburban supermarket. Damien's death did my head in even more than PJ's had the year before. PJ and I had been close when we were teens, but had gone our separate ways by the time he passed. Damien and I were just starting to get acquainted. Too many dead friends, too many dead ends.

I've partaken in my share of chemical indulgences but heroin was one drug I never cared to try. Though the desired effect—blissful nothingness—has always appealed to me, the act of injecting the drug intravenously scared me to death. When I was a child, maybe seven or eight years old, I stumbled upon an anti-drug pamphlet, most likely discarded by a high-school age student who had no time for propaganda. I didn't read the booklet—I was too young even to contemplate the concept of what being straight meant—but some of the images, including a horrifying sketch of a needle underneath the word heroin, spelled out in a brash, bold font, set me off. I was terrified, yet I couldn't look away and couldn't get the visual out of my head. I started drawing pictures of kids shooting up, including a quite elaborate one of a boy walking alongside a railroad track, needle gleefully stuck into his vein. I kept these drawings in a folder on top of the dresser in my bedroom. One day the folder was gone; the evidence discarded. My parents didn't say anything to me, but I got the hint.

When I was old enough to get exposed to drugs, I opted for safer choices. Initially alcohol, later marijuana, pills, and the occasional hallucinogenic. Something about heroin always appealed to me, however, which is probably why I've always veered to music made by junkies: Velvet Underground, Spacemen 3, Rolling Stones when Keith was strung out. The only needle I needed was the one on the grooves.

I get up and decide to have a wander. I'm hungry but apathetic, too listless to even eat. The depression is kicking in and I'm starting to panic again, like I did on my walk from the station. I need to ice my nerves with a stiff drink. I have a quick pint at a pub near the hotel, but the place is noisy, full of obnoxious Dutch heavy metal fans on a bender. I find an upscale wine bar, a lost relic from the eighties when they were trendy for about five minutes. I take a seat on a stool near the end of the bar, as far away from anyone as I can get and order a glass of red. Duran Duran's on the stereo, their comeback hit "Ordinary World." I was never a huge fan of the group apart from a few of the early singles, but the glossy windswept sound helps lighten my mood. Rock 'n' roll saves lives, I think to myself.

I feel a tap on my shoulder. A year ago, nearly to this day, it was Dave who recognized me at the Columbia Hotel. This time the voice is female. It's Siobhan. I get up to greet her and we hug for what feels like an eternity. I can't stop looking at her. She looks so beautiful, so grown-up now. She used to live in jeans and T-shirts, but tonight she's wearing a sleek, figure-hugging dress.

"Drew, I can't believe it's you. I can't believe you didn't tell me you were in Dublin."

"I didn't know I would be here until yesterday. I was in Belfast for a month."

"Something to do with Claire?"

"Something like that. It's a long story, but I don't want to depress you. You look great. Special occasion?"

"No, I'm just out with a few girlfriends. My mum is watching Francis tonight." She points to a group of three other girls, laughing and drinking at a nearby table.

"So what happened with Claire?" she asks.

"Are you sure I'm not keeping you from your friends?" I can't help but notice that one of them is throwing me daggers.

"It's okay," she says.

I give her a quick rundown.

"That's so awful," Siobhan says. "It's like something out of a gruesome gothic novel."

"Part of me wonders if that was her intent. She's quite the literary person when she wants to be."

"Are you going to be okay?" she asks.

"I don't know," I say, trying not to sound melodramatic. "I feel like I'm a bit out of my element."

"You've had a huge shock.

"So what about you? How's Francis? What's going on with Pat?"

"Francis is fine. He's a little darling. Don't remind me of Pat."

"Sorry."

"He's got a new lady friend in Los Angeles of all places for fuck's sake," she says. "Talk about clichés."

"Someday I'll kick his head in for you, but I think half of Dublin might beat me to it."

She smiles, but I can tell she's dejected. "He does pay child support," she says, "but he's too drawn to that nomadic rock 'n' roll lifestyle to settle down and be a good father."

"Well, good riddance to him then."

"Good riddance," she says. "I'll drink to that."

We clink glasses.

"Are you going to be okay?" I ask.

"Of course," says Siobhan. "You know me..."

"I know," I say, remembering an old conversation. "True Irish blue."

She laughs. "You know me well, Drew."

At this point Sinead O'Connor's "Nothing Compares 2 U" comes on. Prince wrote the song, but Sinead owns it. It's possibly the strongest vocal performance I've ever heard. I never tire of it. I'm not pining for anyone the way that Sinead does for her lost lover– the idea of finding a soulmate feels much too trite for me at this moment in time— but I pine for moments like I enjoyed with Emily, when nothing else seemed to matter. Do you remember the little things we did as I lay with you and you had no regrets?

Just as I'm reminded of Fearghal's lyric, Siobhan asks if I'm going to see Whipping Boy at the Olympia tomorrow.

"I didn't know they were playing. Are you going?"

"No," she says. "I'd like to, but this girl has had enough of the nightlife to last a lifetime. Besides, Pat will probably be there. I hear his new girlfriend is in town for a visit."

"Yuck, but I'll definitely go. I'd like to see Whipping Boy

again."

"Don't hurt Pat too badly," jokes Siobhan.

"I won't."

We've had a few drinks at this point and I haven't had anything to eat since breakfast. I'm wrecked. Siobhan seems to be in a similar predicament. We're at that stage where we're both gazing at each other, wondering what might unfold. There's an obvious connection—chemistry—but one of us needs to make the first move.

I try, telling her I have a room at the Clarence and that maybe we could get a drink at the bar.

"Trust me, Drew, I'd like that so much, but it would be all wrong. You mean too much to me to be a one-night stand. I don't want to remember you that way should we never meet again."

"I suppose you're right," I say, trying to compose myself, a little embarrassed at getting shot down. "I'll always remember you as the girl who got away."

"That has a nice ring," she says with a smile. "Perhaps our paths will cross again another time when our lives are less chaotic. I believe in perhaps."

"I'll drink to that," I say.

The girls decide to go dancing at a club. They invite me, but I can tell that most of them want a girls' night out so I decide to bail. I walk back to the hotel, the cool breeze blowing back my hair. I'm exhausted, the month in Belfast suddenly hitting me like a brick. I'm thirty-one, jobless, and broke. My soon to be ex-wife has tried to kill herself twice. What the fuck does that say about me? The only time I feel good is when I escape into music—"you know his life was saved by rock 'n' roll"—everything else is dull and depressing. I saw a shrink when I was younger—mainly to fake symptoms and score Valium—but this time the pain feels real, almost indescribable. I'm sad about so many things. The thought of moving forward has become such a burden. I don't want to go out like PJ or Damien—or like Claire tried to—but I need some kind of release. Everything has become too damn monotonous for me. Love isn't the drug—I've learned that the hard way too many times. Drugs aren't the drug—they're just a convenient escape—and don't even get me started on religion. Even Bono gave up on Jesus.

I fall asleep and dream of my friends Johnny and Damien. The two never met, but in this scenario we're all together in the common room at Eddington Tower, where I lived when I studied at Essex. We're just sitting around, drinking tea, reading music magazines, shooting the shit, not a care in the world. I excuse myself and suddenly find myself lost in a forest. Eventually, I come across a parked car. The door is open, so I go inside and turn on the radio. Echo and the Bunnymen's "The Cutter" is playing, only this is a weird extended live version that I've never heard before. On the chorus the singer Ian keeps ad libbing, "You couldn't cut the mustard, Drew. You're a lost boy, ain'tcha you Drew?" The song never seems to stop, so, finally, I turn off the radio in frustration and leave. I walk through the forest until I come across a small cottage. I look inside the window. Johnny and Damien are there, drinking tea by the fire. I want to join them, but the front door is too small, just a tiny portal. I try to crawl inside, but I'm too large. Johnny and Damien seem oblivious to my struggle. Eventually, I wake up in a cold sweat, thinking to myself, "I can't go back, can I?" I toss and turn, but can't relax. No sleep to kill the bad dreams.

We Don't Need Nobody Else

The Whipping Boy concert is at the Olympia Theatre, a luxurious venue similar to the Shepherd's Bush Empire where I saw them play with Lou Reed. I'm excited to witness what will undoubtedly be a triumphant homecoming gig after a summer playing festivals. I arrive early, hoping to catch the soundcheck, maybe even procure a few choice quotes to use in a follow-up piece for Alternative Press, or possibly Spin, when Whipping Boy breaks America. Surely, it's only a matter of time.

The guys are outside having a smoke. Paul does a double take when he sees me and laughs. "I guess we should never be surprised when you turn up for a gig, Drew."

"Perfect timing," I say. "I just happened to be in town. I didn't know you were playing until yesterday."

"How long are you here for?" asks Myles.

"Not long. I'm flying back to Boston on Monday. I was in Belfast, sorting out things."

"Ah," says Paul. "Claire things?"

"Yeah."

"How is she?"

"Not well," I say. "It's a long story, but it doesn't end well."

"Must be something in the air," says Fearghal. "Columbia just dropped us."

"Fuck," I say. "That sucks. I thought things had been going well."

"Well for us, I suppose," says Fearghal. "Not well for Columbia."

"The person who signed us no longer works for the label. You've no doubt heard that song and dance a few times, Drew," says Paul.

"For sure," I say. "That's awful news. Sorry to hear that."

"It's actually not so bad," says Paul. "We signed a two album deal, so they had to pay us off for the second album that they didn't want to release."

"We'll keep plugging away," says Fearghal. "We don't need nobody else."

We all laugh, but I can tell that getting dropped from Columbia is a major blow. The guys don't seem as excited and inspired as they did that magical evening I saw them in London with Lou Reed. I follow Whipping Boy inside for the soundcheck. They work their way through a few numbers, including a powerful take of "We Don't Need Nobody Else," which seems especially cathartic in light of recent events. While *Heartworm* is flawless from start to finish, "We Don't Need Nobody Else" is definitely the album's centerpiece—their "Do It Clean," their "How Soon is Now?" I let my mind wander to a happier, more innocent time, remembering an Echo and the Bunnymen gig I saw at this very same venue back in 1987 with Damien. This was a few months before Claire and I moved back to America, a few weeks before Damien died.

Claire had gone off to visit her parents for the weekend, so I decided to stay with Damien at his city center flat. It was early evening and we were drinking cans of lager with some of Damien's mates, listening to music; good craic as they like to say in Ireland.

"Should we head to the Underground?" asked one of Damien's friends.

"Just waiting on Will," said Damien.

I wondered who this Will character was when, five minutes later, Will Sergeant from Echo and the Bunnymen walked through the door. Holy fuck. I had no idea that Damien knew Will, that they were actually friends. Our little entourage made our way to the Underground where Into Paradise were playing. Back then they were known as Backwards Into Paradise. The people at the club were in awe of Damien that night as he made the rounds introducing Will to everyone in sight. That's what I remember most about Damien. He was an anti-scenester if you will. He wasn't in it for himself. He wanted everyone to be friends, to bond over the music we all loved. I got to talk to Will a bit that evening and listened attentively as he told me tales of their infamous 1985 Scandinavian tour when the band would get wasted and played covers of old Velvet Underground, Talking Heads, and Rolling Stones songs. He made a dig about Ian McCulloch not being able to hold his drink.

The next morning I was sprawled out on Damien's couch, nursing a hangover, when I heard a loud knock on the door. Damien beat me to the door, greeting Will Sergeant in his underwear, cup of tea in his hand.

"Come on you lazy tossers," said Will. "I want to see some record stores before we do our soundcheck."

Damien and I dressed in a hurry and we spent the rest of the morning showing Will the sights. I still remember

Will barely containing his excitement when he found the "Secret Police" 45 by the sixties garage group the Belfast Gypsies. I tried to grill Damien on how he had become so friendly with Will, but he just shrugged it off, like Will was just another one of his many friends who lived for rock 'n' roll.

"It's a long story," he said. "Maybe some other time."

There never was another time. I was out of sorts at the funeral. It was like I was mourning two friends at the same time. I was in England when PJ died, so I missed his service. In retrospect, I was also mourning my magical friendship with Johnny. The two of us hung out every day for seven months before he returned to the States and I moved to Dublin with Claire. I was deeply in love with Claire back then, but I still needed a close friend, someone who understood my obsession with music. I thought that Damien would fill that void. There was a lot I didn't know about Damien—his heroin problem being the most obvious—but, nevertheless, we had one of those connections that I've experienced with only a handful of people.

The Whipping Boy gig is excellent. Since they're the headliners, they play twice as long as they did when they supported Lou Reed. I don't know if it's because of the recent Columbia news, but the energy tonight is angry and defiant. Early material like "Switchblade Smile" and "I Think I Miss You" sounds almost punk rock, Fearghal rapidly spitting out his words as Paul, Myles, Colm, and Killian forge a brutal wall of sound behind him. They close the set with "We Don't Need Nobody Else" and the audience goes crazy. Never mind Columbia Records, never mind breaking America like U2 did; Whipping Boy are making music on their own terms and they're leaving it up to us to embrace it or walk away.

The mood is quiet backstage. Everyone is having a good time, but the vibe is much different than it was at the Lou Reed show, when everything felt possible. Pat the Almighty is making the rounds, telling anyone who will listen about the new Flash album and their forthcoming U.S. tour. It feels like he's rubbing salt in Whipping Boy's wounds by bringing up America. His girlfriend, an impossibly thin model named Gem, is with him, looking bored and vacant. She holds Pat's hand as if she's an accessory; eye candy for an up and coming rock star.

"Still living in Boston, Drew?" asks Pat the Almighty.

"For now," I say, trying not to let myself get drawn into a conversation. I never liked the guy and now that he's abandoned Siobhan and Francis, I downright hate him.

"We're going to be doing a little tour in a few months. Boston, New York, L.A., and San Francisco."

"Congrats," I say.

"Would love to see you there. Maybe you could write about us. New Irish hope and all that."

"Maybe," I say.

"Shame about Whipping Boy," he says a tad too gleefully. "They approached it all wrong. You need to play the game, do what the label wants at all times if you want to make it in the biz." I hate the way he says biz, effecting a faux Bono transatlantic accent.

"What would you know, Pat. Your record's shite. The only good thing you've ever done is father a wonderful kid, and now you've fucked that up."

Pat looks startled and drops his can of lager. I wonder if

he'll confront me—maybe shove me like Liam Gallagher did to Johnny backstage at the Oasis concert—but he just bends down to pick up the remnants of his drink, and I walk away.

There's a small party for Whipping Boy at the Clarence later in the evening, just family and friends. I'm touched when Paul invites me, thanking me for always believing in the music. I have a few beers and feel loose. I'm having a great time, regretting that I booked my return ticket. I don't have anything keeping me in Dublin anymore, but I've burned all my bridges in Boston, too. This has been the most trying year of my life, yet I've managed to survive. What doesn't kill you, only makes you stronger, or something like that. PJ didn't make it, nor did Damien. The verdict's still out on Claire. As for me, right now I feel like I'm going to be okay, that I'll find a way to pull through. Rock 'n' roll saves lives, I think to myself once again.

I go outside to get some air. I see Fearghal. I thought he had left the party, but he's standing on the sidewalk, smoking a cigarette. I nod to him, trying to gauge his mood, hoping he won't be angry and blow up at me. My confrontation with Pat the Almighty was enough entertainment for the evening. Fearghal nods back. He looks lost and withdrawn, like he could use some company, so I approach him and bum a cigarette.

"Didn't know you smoked," Fearghal says.

"I usually don't, but I could really use one right now to ice my nerves." I tell him about my scuffle with Pat the Almighty.

"I hate him," says Fearghal, "but he's nothing to get worked up about. He's an untalented wanker who tries far too hard to please."

"Sadly, he's the kind of person record labels seem to love. It's a sickening business."

"It is," says Fearghal, "except for the music."

"True," I say. I take a long drag from my cigarette, trying to think of something else to say.

"So you're heading back to America then?" Fearghal asks.

"Yeah. Claire and I are getting divorced. She kind of lost her mind."

"Love does that to you. It can make you do crazy things."

I nod in agreement and take another drag. "What about you, Fearghal? What's next for Whipping Boy?"

"We'll keep making music. Our new songs are better. Just wait until you hear them."

His tone sounds defiant, but a little forced, like he's trying to convince himself. It crosses my mind that getting dropped by a label is like getting dumped by a woman. No matter how much you might believe in yourself, or your music, it's impossible not to let seeds of doubt creep inside.

At this point a limousine slowly pulls up to the hotel entrance. The driver gets out and opens the back door. Out spill three drunken, scantily clad girls, who can barely keep their composure. By their looks, they are no doubt returning from a raucous hen party or, perhaps, a crazy night at the club. One of girls slips and crashes hard on her back, dropping and shattering a bottle of bubbly. The other two giggle and try to lift their friend from the ground to no avail. U2 is blaring loudly on the car stereo—"Even Better Than The Real Thing"—as the driver comes over to aid the fallen girl, finally escorting her to the entrance as her two friends stumble behind. Fearghal and I can't stop laughing. The driver turns his head and smiles. He's seen it all before.

Fearghal lights up another cigarette. He asks if I want one, but I decline.

"So do you think Whipping Boy will ever be the soundtrack to a hen party gone wrong?" I ask.

"Ha, never."

"It's a shame that you're not big like U2 though. Your records are better. Do you ever get jealous about stuff like that?"

"You can't think that way or it will drive you mad."

"I guess you're right. Whipping Boy aren't really a limousine band, anyway," I say.

Fearghal nods in agreement and jokes, "A band's always happiest when it's carrying its own gear."

Gimme Danger

I came back to Boston expecting the worst—a scolding from my brother, perhaps even an intervention from my parents, but everyone was surprisingly sympathetic about my impulsive Irish misadventure. Everyone, except Nick Danger.

I called Nick a few days after landing at Logan and got directed straight to voice mail. The next day, a very young, overly zealous, bubbly girl from Spin called, saying that Nick wanted me to interview Ocean Colour Scene for an upcoming feature. I said sure. I don't like the group much, but I needed the money, especially if a move to New York was still in the cards. It was probably the most miserable half hour of work I've endured since I washed dishes at a Chinese restaurant back in high school. The interview took place backstage at a dingy dive bar venue in Cambridge called TT The Bear's Place. The band were full of themselves, like they were the second coming of the Who, constantly complaining about the small size of the venue, as if I had the power to transport them to the fucking Boston Garden.

"We play arenas in England, mate," said the guitarist Steve in a faux working class accent. "D'you know what I mean?"

Steve kept namedropping his 'mate' Paul Weller, reminding me several times that he's also in Weller's touring group, perhaps a desperate ploy to cull some cred in their attempt to break America, like Blur and Oasis have already done.

The concert was truly awful. The band strutted out on stage to Booker T and the M.G.'s shit hot instrumental "Green Onions," but it all went downhill fast once they performed their dire sixties revival originals. A few years ago, Ocean Colour Scene were much more psychedelic, trying to be the next Stone Roses or House of Love; now they were jumping on the Britpop train. They had the mod look, but it was sloppy compared to the manicured style cultivated by Menswear. I felt like I was watching the musical equivalent of Civil War recreationists—jumped-up mods with vintage guitars, in place of old men in beards, playing war games in the fields.

The crowd seemed to be eating it up though; lots of young kids in the audience, jumping up and down and screaming. I half expected to find Emily up front, dancing to the music, hand in hand with Ryan, before remembering that she was gone.

The next day I sucked it up and typed up a passable feature and emailed it to Nick. Nick called me back with some edits.

"You're being a little snarky there in places," he said in a tone that was much more boss than old friend.

"Kind of hard to write about a band I hate. There are a few decent soundbites in there. It's good enough." Nick's phone demeanor put me in a defensive mood.

"I'll make it work," said Nick. "Hey, we just got a new CD that might be up your alley. They're a new Dublin group called Flash. Kind of a cross between Radiohead and early U2. They're playing in Boston soon. I can get you on the guest list."

I groaned, perhaps too loudly, reminded of my not so

pleasant encounter with Pat the Almighty.

"Oh God, anyone but Flash."

"I thought you might like them," said Nick, sounding a little hurt.

"The music's okay, I suppose, but they're such wankers. I knew them when I lived in Dublin. It just ticks me off that it's them who are about to break America and not Whipping Boy. Flash are one of those groups that are built and designed to sell out, not have a career."

"It's a cruel industry, Drew. It's about winners and losers. There's no room for anyone in between. You know that." Nick was sounding more like a stockbroker than the journalist I idolized ten years ago, the one who inspired me to make a career out of rock 'n' roll.

"Start a fanzine if you want to champion underdogs," Nick continued. "I've got magazines to sell if I want to keep my job… and I have plenty of other writers that would jump at the chance to interview Flash if you don't want to." For some reason the image of a fat middle manager in a cheap suit came into my head. I imagined said manager telling some young kid just out of college, "Look at me. This could be you in another twenty years."

"Look, I'm sorry Nick. I've had a tough month. I could use a fresh start. Is that Spin job still in the cards?"

Silence, at least twenty seconds of uncomfortable silence that felt like minutes, before Nick finally said, "Sorry mate, I didn't think you were still interested. I've hired someone else."

"Christ, Nick! Why didn't you just ask me?"

"Well, Drew, you kind of just fucked off to Ireland, didn't you?"

"Yeah, you kind of do that when your wife tries to kill herself, Nick."

"Sorry, Drew, I really am. I'll keep you in mind if something pops up." He sounded stupidly posh, like Hugh Grant. I wanted to punch him.

"Don't bother," I said before slamming down the receiver.

My first inclination after getting off the phone was to raid Paul's wine collection, but I decided to finish unpacking instead. I had asked my mom to mail me some things from my old bedroom in Michigan when I thought I would be moving to New York. I go through a box of books and stumble across a dog-eared paperback of Nik Cohn's 1969 history of rock 'n' roll, preposterously titled *Awopbopaloobop Alopbamboom* as a tribute to Little Richard's primal scream on "Tutti Frutti." Cohn was the first famous British rock critic, who retired at the ridiculously young age of twenty-two, moving on to more literary endeavors, including a story that would later be worked into the film *Saturday Night Fever*. I remember being struck by an interview where Cohn said he got out of rock 'n' roll at such a young age because he wanted to stay true to its roots and remember it for what it should be: a doomed romance and not something to get rich off of.

I crack open a box of vinyl and hold a worn copy of the Stooges *Raw Power* album in my hands, allowing memories of why I truly love music, despite all the heartbreak it can bring, to pour back. A lot of my favorite artists are destined to be footnotes in the annals of rock 'n' roll. Others, like the Stooges and Velvet Underground, eventually got the credit they deserved. I think about my Irish friends,

Whipping Boy. Will time be kind to them? I close the curtains, dim the lights, and play *Heartworm* for the first time since returning from Ireland, embracing the doomed romance of it all. I don't need anybody else.

That Was Then, This Is Now

My brother takes me in when the Spin position falls through. I find a new job at Harvard. Outsiders have this romanticized view of the institution, but the joke amongst students there is that the hardest part of Harvard is getting admitted; that the actual workload is no different to that of a state school. As far as working for the university goes, it's no different to any other office work I've done, ivory tower elitists be damned. My new position is quite similar to what I did at Cooperation North, only this time I'm helping people in Latin America, not Ireland. I'm seeing a shrink several days a week—not Emily's mom—and she's helping me work things out. I smile at some of the memories, others make me cringe and cry. I just want to freeze frame the happy stuff and stay static. Moving forward scares me. Paul suggests I go to AA and do the twelve steps thing—not the first or last time someone has said those words to me—but I don't think I'm one of the shiny happy people who can sail through life without chemical assistance.

Older people tell me that things get better in your late thirties—or even after that—but I don't believe that's true. I'm not happy. I'm stable. I think that's why so many rock stars—or fellow travelers like Damien and PJ—check out so young. Rock 'n' roll is a young man's game, and some of us aren't cut out to be grown-ups. It's not in our DNA. Right now I'm at an awkward stage. I feel too old to die young and too young to die now.

Paul bought me a copy of *High Fidelity* for Christmas. "It's so you," he kept saying. It was an enjoyable read and I suppose I could see his point, but I hated the way Rob ended up with a lawyer girlfriend and Barry turned his experimental noise band into a boomer nostalgia covers act. It ended on too positive of a note. Nick Danger got his *High Fidelity* ending when he married his lawyer wife, but life doesn't work that way for most of us music guys.

I wonder what I'll do with my life now that I've temporarily fucked up my journalism career. I know that I'll eventually need a creative outlet to impede depression and the vices that go along with it. I think about Whipping Boy and Fearghal in particular. There's a hidden track at the end of *Heartworm* called "A Natural," where he candidly describes his recent diagnosis as a paranoid schizophrenic. It makes me think of Claire and all her ghosts. Despite Fearghal's struggles, he vows to move on, telling us near the end that he's met a new girl. One can feel a sense of hope until Fearghal proclaims at the end: "I myself am heaven and hell." I suppose we all are.

Emily phones just after New Year's. "Please don't hang up," she says.

"I won't," I say.

"I've wanted to call you for like forever, but I keep chickening out. I finally found the courage." I can tell she's nervous. Her voice is shaking and I can tell that she's pacing the floor.

"You're the last person I expected to hear from," I say.

"Don't be mad, Drew. Please don't. I just want to say I'm sorry. I was such a bitch to you. I should have never left… I'm home now."

"For winter break?"

"No, for good. I came back a few weeks ago."

"What happened?"

"Ryan beat the shit out of me. That's what happened." She begins to cry.

"Jesus, I'm sorry. What an asshole. I hope the cops roughed him up."

"I didn't press charges," she says. "I just left. After he hit me, I packed up a small suitcase and took a cab to the airport. I bought a standby ticket. I left everything behind: my job, my stuff, most of my clothes."

"It's not my business, but Ryan's getting off far too easy."

"I didn't want to deal. I needed to get out. He won't bother me again. He shipped my stuff home the next day. I told him never to call me again and he hasn't. He's an asshole, but he's not stupid."

"Did he ever hurt you before?"

"Just with words. Our relationship never worked after I told him about us. He said he forgave me, but he always threw it back in my face. We'd get intimate and then he'd ask if he was better in bed than you were. He got really drunk and called me a whore the night he beat me up. I had to lock myself in the bathroom. He kept trying to kick the door down before he passed out. It was awful."

"God, I'm so sorry. I wish you'd told me sooner."

"I thought you hated me. I cry every time I think about that day you walked away. I kept hoping you would at least look back at me."

"I don't hate you. How could I?"

"I'm sorry, Drew. I'm sorry for everything. I'm a mess."

"It's okay," I say. "Where are you now?"

"I'm with my mom and dad. I'm not doing anything. I don't have a job and I don't have any friends here. I feel like a little kid again. I kind of failed at being a grown-up."

"Growing up is overrated."

She laughs. "That's why I love you, Drew. You know how to live for the moment."

I don't say anything, surprised to hear her say she loves me. Surprised that she thinks I have a positive outlook on life.

"Are you still there, Drew?"

"Yeah," I say. "Sometimes I feel like I just brought you down, Emily. Like I fucked up everything for you. You'd probably be happy in California right now if you hadn't met me."

"That's not true," she says. "You were like the best thing to happen to me. I could have stayed there. I made friends at the newspaper. I liked my job, but I liked the idea of maybe seeing you again more."

She sighs. "Are you okay, Drew? What's new?"

I tell her everything. We stay on the phone for hours.

"Can I see you, again?" she asks.

"Like right now?" I laugh.

"No, silly, it's like 3:00am, but soon. It's your birthday this week, isn't it?"

"Yeah, tomorrow. Well, actually today now."

"Happy birthday, Drew."

We make plans to meet at Casablanca in Harvard Square. I arrive early and have a quick walk around. The restaurant portion is upscale, but the dimly lit bar in back has a seedier vibe, full of Harvard professors and foreign students slumming it for the evening. I feel at home, like I've been here before. Maybe it's the jukebox full of old classics, the kind of stuff Loren and I used to listen to. Elvis, Rolling Stones, Isaac Hayes, Leonard Cohen. Music for drinkers.

I walk to the bar and notice Jethro standing behind the counter, mixing a cocktail. It's been close to six months since I've been to the Red Dragon and I'm startled to see him in new settings.

"Jethro, how's it going, man? What are you doing here?"

He cuts me off with an indignant look and says, "My name's not Jethro. I'm Kenny."

"Sorry, man. I thought you were someone else."

"No worries, chief. What can I get you?"

I order a glass of red and take a small sip before I lose myself in thought, trying to figure out what just happened.

I feel a tap on my shoulder and turn around. It's Emily. She drapes her overcoat on the chair next to mine and sits down. She's wearing a black dress and sunglasses. The contrast of her ghostly white skin against the blood red vintage makes me think of a vampire drawing blood. Emily removes her shades, revealing a faded bruise underneath her right eye. I flinch, but she just smiles and says, "Hey, you."

Lightning Source UK Ltd.
Milton Keynes UK
UKHW040634010520
362627UK00001B/72

9 781937 513726